The Lies that Bind

D.L. Sparks

URBAN Renaissance

www.urbanbooks.net

Urban Books, LLC
1199 Straight Path
West Babylon, NY 11704

ISBN- 13: 978-1-60162-200-6
ISBN- 10: 1-60162-200-7

First Printing January 2010
Printed in the United States of America

10 9 8 7 6 5 4 3 2 1

*This is a work of fiction. Any references or similarities to
actual events, real people, living, or dead, or to real locales
are intended to give the novel a sense of reality. Any
similarity in other names, characters, places, and incidents
is entirely coincidental.*

Distributed by Kensington Publishing Corp.
Submit Wholesale Orders to:
Kensington Publishing Corp.
C/O Penguin Group (USA) Inc.
Attention: Order Processing
405 Murray Hill Parkway
East Rutherford, NJ 07073-2316
Phone: 1-800-526-0275
Fax: 1-800-227-9604

Dedication

For Monica Renee Bowie
You are loved and truly missed.
Missing since July 5, 2007

Acknowledgments

Okay, so I get an e-mail requesting my Dedication and Acknowledgments. I double-check to make sure that the e-mail is addressed to me, and that I'm not dreaming and . . . I'm not. That's when it hits me. Wow! It's happening. My baby is about to be born (published) and presented to the world. So, after picking myself up off the floor, I better get busy.

"For I know the plans I have for you," declares the Lord, "plans to prosper you & not harm you, plans to give you hope and a future."

Jeremiah 29:11

I would like to give thanks, first and foremost, to God for giving me such an awesome gift in writing. Who would've thought that the love I have for reading would grow into what it has today. God is truly awesome!

Second, I want to thank . . . UGH! I hate that cliché. Let's try something different. Okay, I wanna give a shout-out to few people who have stuck with me during my journey to bring you this novel.

To my husband, Ronnie, thank you for all your love and support . . . even when I didn't deserve it.

To my babies, Taylor, RJ, and Joshua, you will always be the reason I do what I do.

Acknowledgments

To my mom, thanks for being you, and allowing me to be me.

To my brother, Chris, your movie selections still suck, but I love you anyway.

To my cousin, Nicky, you're my idol in so many ways, and you don't even know it. I love you!

To my wonderful agent, Portia, thank you, thank you, thank you, for believing in my abilities, and me. Thank you for helping me stay focused and seeing the next book even before I finished the first.

I definitely want to thank my new family at Urban Books. I look forward to a great relationship, and many, many bestsellers.

Tia, there is nothing that can be put into words that will ever express how much I love you, and appreciate God bringing you into my life. Who would've thought that I would find my sister on the other side of a hospital wall?

Terren Grimble, you are a true friend, and an awesome writer! I enjoyed *Love Lessons,* and if you ever stop obsessing over the font for *Life Lessons*, I'm sure I'll love that too!

To my literary twin, Péron F. Long, thanks for keeping me laughing, and focused, but most of all, thank you for being you, and for being a friend; even when you didn't have to be. And to that question you keep asking me, the answer is still NO!

Tina Brooks-McKinney, you have been a blessing to me in this big old world. I love you to death for your support, and your friendship.

Oh, wait, gotta do this: "I want to give thanks to that incredibly awesome, kick-ass, not special in the little yellow bus way girl, Raeha!" (I said it just like you told me to!) But, you know, it's true, girl. You're one of the coolest friends I've never met! I promise I will get to Austin soon.

Acknowledgments

Sharon Denny, thank you so much for being you. I wish you much literary success, sis!

To my girl, Mo Flames, still waiting on that tour, chica! I'm ready to set the South on fire because you know, "where's there's Sparks . . . there's Flames!"

To Dorien, the Yin to my Yang. Thank you so much for being a true friend, keeping me focused, picking me up, and dusting me off when I got derailed. I promise we'll be on the beach soon sipping vanilla vodka and ginger ale!

To Lisha, thanks for reading this and helping me get it right. Above all else, thanks for being a friend.

Now, I need to thank Chanel. I love you so much for your enormous heart, and your awesome spirit. I look forward to what God has in store for you because I know it is huge!

Thank you, Keysha, for always checking on me and making sure I haven't pulled out all my hair. Thanks for planning all those awesome girls' only weekends that I swear I am gonna start making it to sometime soon.

To Robin, the best friend that I never see! Girl, you know you just live too far away.

To all the book clubs and reviewers, thank you! There would be no "us" without "you."

To my family at Black Writers With A Purpose, thank you for all your support and laughs. I'm glad I have you in my corner!

To my Facebook family, much love! You guys keep me laughing and on my toes with them dang quizzes!

And, most of all, I would like to thank YOU! Yes, you . . . the one reading this. I hope you enjoyed the peek I gave you into these characters' lives. I hope they stick with you long after you've put the book down!

Please log on to my website: www.dlsparks.com or send me an e-mail at author@dlsparks.com. You can also find me on MySpace at www.myspace.com/authordlsparks.

Acknowledgments

Well, I gotta go. I'm off to meet a friend for lunch at the Cheesecake Factory! If I have forgotten anyone, please charge it to my head, and not to my heart!

Your girl,

D.L.Sparks

The Butterfly Effect

The Essence of Chaos . . . not the movie.

"Thou Shalt Not Commit Adultery . . ."

Exodus 20:14

Chapter One

You ever notice how stress destroys an atmosphere?

The way it sucks the life right out of a room? Wine doesn't taste as sweet, blues are less blue, and flowers don't have a smell. That's exactly how I felt when I found out my husband had been cheating on me. It was as if time froze, and suddenly my colorful world was starkly black and white.

Surprised, no. And I guess it's because I counsel women almost daily who have cheating husbands, so infidelity to me was as common as some young child star going off to rehab.

But was I pissed? Hell, yes!

The fact that he had carried on the affair for the better part of a year is what pissed me off the most. A whole year. That's 365 days of lies, sneaking around, and broken promises. Cheating happened to other women, not me. When my friends cried on my shoulder about their men cheating, I just smiled and told them it would be okay; that good men are out there. I assured them that my husband and I had been going strong for over seven years and he had never cheated on me. Well, never say never.

"Teri. Are you listening to me?"

My husband's voice snapped me out of my trip to

the past. The sights and sounds from inside Paschal's Restaurant came back into focus, dragging me back to reality. I looked at Donovan, searched his face for the man I fell in love with. The man with Latin roots so deep he couldn't help but speak Spanish when he got angry. The man with a river of love that raged so loud, sometimes the roar was deafening.

Deep down I knew his affair had nothing to do with whether or not he loved me. It had a lot more to do with how I made him feel the last couple of years. He made that perfectly clear.

"Yes, Donovan, I heard you. You're not happy, so you want a divorce," I snapped. "Your actions have been screaming that for weeks. We barely talk anymore, and we never spend any time together. Hell, we don't even sleep in the same bed!"

He tossed his napkin on the table, and fire rose in his eyes. "I guess you didn't hear me, because that is not what I said!" He blew out some air. "Damn, Teri! I am not a patient, so stop trying to analyze me."

"Look, you just told me you are unhappy in our marriage; what other conclusion can I get from that?"

"How about asking me why, instead of coming up with your own ending?"

"Why? You seem to have already made up your mind."

His posture softened, like the weight of the world rested on his broad shoulders. He looked worn. Almost as worn as I felt. The past two years, we just couldn't seem to connect. It was like something had reached back in time and derailed our happily ever after. We were almost like roommates.

Roommates who wished they lived alone.

I started working longer hours, and he compensated for my absence by doing the same. Being a psychologist, I knew better, but before everything else, I am only human, and I withdrew into my work. I figured it was easier to submerge my energy into solving my patients' problems rather than my own.

I sat back and crossed my arms against my chest. My eyes met my husband's, and I absorbed his frustration. "Is this about Tracie?"

His beautiful face twisted into a disgusted frown as he let out a heavy sigh. He ran his hand over his jet black curls, and then slammed the table with his fist. "This has nothing to do with her! *Damn*, you just don't get it, do you?"

"Well, what else am I supposed to think?"

"So there couldn't possibly be anything wrong with *you*? It has to be someone else's fault, is that it?"

"That's not fair, Donovan."

The waitress walked over, forcing us to swallow whatever argument was on the tips of our tongues. After she finished filling our water glasses, she made her way back into the sea of diners. I looked across the table at my husband. We were at an impasse.

His affair affected me more than I wanted to admit to him or anyone else—not even to my best friend, Renee.

I took a deep breath. "I don't understand what you want from me."

"I am trying to get you to talk to me!" he said, his voice rising, but just as quickly lowering. "Why can't you see that?"

"I do see that."

He let out a sigh. "I can't tell. I'm your husband; I need more from you than what you are offering."

He backed down for a second, taking his argument back to his side of the table. I took a sip of my water and tried to calm my nerves.

I hated the fact that that bitch had etched a permanent spot in our history. Ever since I found out about his affair, our marriage had steadily worsened. Especially considering how long he had denied it and

3

told me it was my imagination, only for me to find out that a year of suspicion had been justified.

I don't like being lied to. In my eyes, when you lie to me, you take away my choice. My choice as to how I wanted to deal with a situation. He took that away from me, and made me a pawn in his game without asking me how I felt about it, without so much as a "thank you" or a "fuck you."

I leaned forward in my chair. "What do you want from me, Donovan?"

"For you to either work on this marriage or get out of it."

That hit me like a right hook from Mike Tyson. I didn't know whether to fight back or throw in the towel. The ringing of my cell phone made the decision for me. My electronic leash was more like a choke chain. Donovan's eyes shot to the phone vibrating on the table, then back to me.

"Are you going to answer it?"

"You know I have to. What if it's a patient?"

"No, you don't. You're answering it because you want to."

"Come on, Donovan!"

He pushed away from the table and stood up. "Answer the phone, Dr. McCall."

Before I could say anything, he threw a hundred dollar bill on the table, and disappeared through the glass doors. I knew what that meant—him sleeping in the guest room and me alone in our master bedroom, again. I looked to the door that my husband had just walked through, and then back to the phone. At this point, work was easier to deal with; anything was easier than trying to bag the puff of smoke that had become my marriage.

Chapter Two

"Martin needs you to come in today around two. He wants to meet with you."

This was one of the downsides to being a psychologist, being on call. Whether it was a patient or my boss, my phone never seemed to stop. So I guess after almost four years of this, I could see how Donovan could be so frustrated with my work, but I really wished he would understand that I loved what I did.

The phone call that cut our lunch short was from Eva, my secretary. She had to be the most annoying little thing in the office. I tried not to complain too much, considering she was the fourth temp that the agency had sent me in the last two months. The secretary before her couldn't seem to stay off the phone, chatting it up with her baby's father, and the one before that openly admitted that she was into the occult; so she definitely had to go. The one before her had no sense of time, and was late every day. When she finally did show up, she could barely open up a Word document. So now, I was on Eva. I wanted her to work out just because I was tired of learning a new name every couple of weeks.

I looked at my watch. It was almost one.

"Okay, well, I need you to call my two o'clock and push them back to three, and reschedule my three o'clock all together."

My three o'clock was Mr. Wendell. He had a fear

of clowns that was wearing me out over the past few weeks. Just when I thought we were having a break-through, he up and tries to go to his niece's birthday party where there just happened to be clowns. Lots and lots of clowns. He was in my office crying long past his allotted hour that week.

"No problem, Dr. McCall," Eva said. "And someone named Darienne has called twice for you."

I thought about that name. It didn't sound familiar.

"A new patient?"

"She didn't say. But she said she'd try you later."

"Thanks."

I dialed Renee on my way to the office. Renee and I had been friends since forever. She was that one friend I could talk to once a month, and it was as if we just spoke the night before. She was a controller at a huge accounting firm downtown, and her husband was in the military. He had recently gotten orders for deployment to Germany by the end of the year, so they had been spending a lot of time together, which meant less girl talk for us.

Derrick finally answered, and told me Renee was at the library. He immediately started in on me about the season tickets for the Falcon games that were collecting dust in my den. He had been angling for them ever since I told him Donovan and I rarely go anymore. Sometimes, Donovan would go and take a client, but for the most part, he watched the games at home because we subscribed to DIRECTV's *NFL Sunday Ticket*.

I continued, "Tell her to call me at the office, and I will see what I can do about the tickets."

"A'ight. Thanks."

I definitely wasn't up for working today. It was a beautiful late June day; the city was on fire. The sky was cloud free, and a beautiful, piercing shade of blue.

This was the kind of weather where you could

drop the top on your car and ride up I-85, admiring the mountains and reveling in the beauty of God, not go to some closed-in office space listening to other people's problems. Most days I loved going to work. I have always been fascinated with why people do the things they do, as well as the inner workings of a person. If someone could crack that code, it would make the world a better place. However, my first love was dancing. Unfortunately, while in college, I realized that pirouettes and toe touches didn't pay the bills, so my focus changed from dance to psychology.

On the outside, it appeared I had it all. Lucrative salary, wardrobe that any female would want, friends on the four corners of the U.S., and a husband fine enough to make *People* magazine's sexiest man alive self-conscious. Donovan was a perfect blend of his Latin and African-American roots with a philanthropic nature that everyone loved about him.

Ever since his affair, our sex life had been non-existent. A woman in her early thirties should be swinging from a chandelier, not faking sleep so her husband wouldn't touch her. We hadn't had sex in almost two weeks. Don't get me wrong, I was still attracted to him, but every time we managed to get the fire high enough to consummate, I would picture him with her. Then, all I could do was lay there and hope he would pull a quickie on me. It had been six months since I'd found out about the affair, and it was a wound that was slow to heal. When we made the decision to try to save our marriage, it seemed so easy.

Now, I wasn't so sure.

When I finally made it to the office, the place was buzzing.

Lunch had been catered, and people who otherwise didn't speak were gathered around the conference room chatting it up as if it were a family reunion. A few people were hovering by the punch bowl. I noticed Eva munching on what appeared to be a ham sandwich. I tried to see her as more than a glorified secretary, but when you come to work with bright red hair and talons for nails, it's really hard to see anything else.

I walked down the long hallway that led to my office, and frowned as I opened the door. Don't get me wrong. It was nice by most office standards. The upscale oak furniture and the flat-screen twenty-two inch LCD flat panel monitor situated next to my charging Black-Berry made me feel important. Not to mention the small bathroom that was nestled in the corner near my huge bookcase. That's the one thing, other than the view, that I loved about the office. But more than anything, I felt like a caged animal. I hated having to punch an invisible clock, log hours, and wait for someone else to sign my paycheck. I sank into my chair, inhaled the smell of lavender and chamomile that filled the room from the candles that rested all around my office. It was aromatherapy at its best in here. I needed all the stress relief I could get.

I rolled my eyes at the pink slips of memo paper covering my desk. Instead of putting them in my box like she was supposed to, Eva had tossed them all over my desk. I looked at the picture of Donovan and me on my desk. It was taken during our trip to Mexico to visit where his mother was born.

I was dressed in shorts and a tank top. My hair was a little shorter then, resting on my shoulders. I let it grow out after we got back from the beach, and now it was down my back. Donovan always said I resembled Alicia Keys. I had seen Alicia Keys in concert once; she was taller than I was, and my hair was lighter.

I picked up the picture, and admired my husband. Donovan was wearing a pair of jean shorts and a white Sean John T-shirt. His tanned skin and dark eyes punctuated his exotic look.

I turned around and opened my blinds. I admired

the city, taking in the energy that Atlanta gave off. It was an energy that enticed people from all walks of life, and all kinds of backgrounds to move here to make something of themselves.

"What are you doing here?" A voice came from behind me.

I spun around in my chair, and smiled at my coworker, Harrison Jeffries.

His broad frame was clad in an Armani suit that looked like it was made just for him. His tie was beautiful, as always, and his smile was intoxicating.

He had tried to convince me many times to meet him for "drinks," but I always came up with an excuse, the main one being that his wife wouldn't appreciate it. She was squeezing out kids so fast, we kept the baby shower decorations on standby just for him.

"Meeting," I said, sifting through my memos.

"Oh, yeah. I heard about that. Weren't you supposed to be off?"

I looked up at him. "Unfortunately. Do you know what the meeting is about?"

"Something to do with billable hours, and HIPAA. You know how they are," he said.

HIPAA, or the Health Insurance Portability and Accountability Act, is the big brother of how healthcare data is exchanged, and the securities in place to protect the privacy of patients. Basically, put in place to keep private things private.

"Didn't we just go over that?" I asked, now scrolling through my e-mails.

"You know, they are trying to make sure we are complying, basically covering their behinds," he said, rubbing his goatee.

I scrunched my nose. "Whatever."

"Well, considering the crazy clients I have, I could probably write a book."

I smiled and stood up. "So, you're the reason for this meeting then?"

He laughed. "Are you coming to the fundraiser?"

"I plan on it."

Then he asked the million dollar question. "Is your husband coming?"

I cleared my throat, picked up my BlackBerry, and pretended I was looking for something. "You know what, I don't know. He's been under the weather lately."

Thankfully, he just smiled and walked out. No words were needed to validate the lie I had just told.

As much as I tried, I couldn't shake Donovan's face. I had tried calling him at his office twice on my way in, and each time, I got his secretary giving me some bull about a meeting.

Other than Donovan, his partner was the only other investment banker in the office, and he traveled more than eighty percent of the time. Donovan was vice president, which was why he made almost seven figures a year plus bonuses. Donovan was responsible for the assets that were primarily in the Southeast and Northeast parts of the United States, his partner handled the Northwest and West Coast accounts. I had only met his partner a few times, but he seemed nice enough. Typical investment banker with a wife, two kids, with a huge bank account to match.

I hit the speed dial button on my BlackBerry and dialed his office. This time he answered.

I let out a sigh. "Hello."

"What's up?"

"I'm sorry, Donovan."

Silence.

"Look, I want our marriage to work just as much as you do, but you have to understand that this is my job."

More silence.

"Are you going to say anything?"

"What do you want me to say? How long am I supposed to play second to your career, Teri? I need a wife."

"Is that why you cheated? Because she gave you attention, stroked your ego, and sucked your dick on command?"

"I am not going there with you right now. We can talk about this when I get home."

"What time will that be?" I asked.

"Around six."

"My last patient is out the door by four; I am home by five. Don't forget about the fundraiser tonight."

"Yeah, okay."

"Are you going or not?"

"I don't know."

I sank back in my chair. "What do you mean you don't know? Either you are or you're not."

"I will see you when I get home."

I disconnected the call, and felt myself getting tense and frustrated. I got up and went into the bathroom to try to pull myself together. Looking at myself in the mirror told the real story that lived behind my brown eyes: hurt, anger, pain, and frustration. I might as well have it tattooed on my forehead. My hair was still neatly tucked in a bun, but my eyes held the truth. I was tired.

When I emerged from my bathroom, Eva was sitting in one of the chairs across from my desk, wearing way too much makeup and some horrid perfume. The black pumps she was wearing were worn, and her skirt was way too short for corporate America. She handed me an envelope and told me it was from my boss, Martin.

"He wants to meet you in his office in five minutes."

I rolled my eyes. The last thing I felt like doing right now was having a closed door session with him. His conversations tended to get long-winded, and I wasn't in the mood for it, not now.

She continued, ignoring my frustration. "And you have a message." She held the pink piece of paper out for me to take.

I grabbed it. That lady Darienne's number was

11

scribbled on the front. I tucked it into the small pocket on the front of my suit jacket, and headed to Dr. Lee's office. I stopped and checked my reflection in the mirrored logo above the secretary's desk before pulling myself together and tapping on his door before entering. I could hear him on the phone, but he motioned for me to come in anyway.

He hung up and gazed at me. "I am glad you could make it. I hope you weren't too put out."

"No, I was already on my way in."

He stepped around his desk and motioned for me to take a seat, and then closed his door. I really got nervous then. All kinds of butterflies took flight in my stomach.

"I don't have a lot of time, so let's get this started," he continued.

I smiled, but didn't say anything.

"Have you had a chance to look in the envelope?"

"Actually, no, I haven't," I said, sliding my finger under the flap and pulling out the thick paper.

"I will help you out," he said, hurrying the meeting along. "It's an offer. An offer that I have put together for the person I would like to be partner in the practice."

I looked at the short man as he maneuvered around his office while he talked. I watched him, but he didn't show any real emotion, and he was all business. All about the practice—billable hours, customer after-care, things like that.

"What does that have to do with me?" I asked absentmindedly.

He stopped at his bookshelf and turned around. "You are the one I want to make partner. I love your work ethic, and the patients love you. The staff really likes you, and you have your head on straight."

It took me a second, but then it hit me like a ton of bricks as I read through the proposal.

This moment was bittersweet in light of what was

going on at home right now. I knew it would mean longer hours and a heavier workload, but I would be gaining the recognition that I'd wanted. Tension settled in as for the first time in a long time, I thought about what my husband would say.

He asked, "Is there a problem?"

"I . . . uh, I am very thankful for the opportunity," I said. "Can I take it home and talk it over with my husband?"

"Sure . . . sure! Of course," he said, waving me off. "Just let me know something by the end of the month."

"Thank you, I will."

I stood up and tried to balance on wobbly legs as I headed toward the lunch in the conference room.

I managed to sidestep a cake that had mysteriously appeared congratulating me, and made my way to my office to call Donovan. I wanted so badly for him to be happy for me, but all he heard was longer hours and more work.

"Teri, I am tired of being married to a memory. You are already stressed enough and bringing work home. How can you think this is a good thing?"

"I know, I know."

"But—" he started.

"But," I said, "it's a great opportunity. Do you want me to turn it down?"

"I want you to do what you want to do; especially since you are going to do that anyway."

"That's not fair, Donovan."

"Teri, why are you doing this? I make enough money to support both of us."

No matter how true that statement was, it still agitated me. I wasn't trying to be taken care of. I enjoyed working, and he knew that. I wasn't trying to be at home barefoot and pregnant, and I know that's what he wanted. That's what his affair was all about. She was there when I wasn't. She listened when I couldn't.

My thoughts went to my medicine cabinet full of

fertility drugs that were a waste of money. I had been to more doctors than I cared to admit, and there was still no bun in the oven. All the doctors kept saying the same thing: Nothing was wrong, it would happen when it should.

"Teri, how are we ever going to start a family if all you do is work?"

"What do you want me to do, Donovan? I can't just quit."

"Why not?"

My other line rang, adding insult to injury.

"Donovan, I will see you when I get home."

He hung up without saying good-bye or congratulations. Flames from anger lapped at my ears. The phone rang, and I snatched it up, inflicting my anger on whoever was the unlucky person on the other end.

Renee asked, "What's wrong with you?"

"Oh, hey. Sorry. What's going on?"

"Are you getting ready to leave?"

"Yeah, I am trying to catch Donovan at home. I have that fundraiser tonight."

"Oh, that's right. Did you find the shoes you were looking for to match your dress?"

"Yeah, I finally found them at Lenox Square Mall."

My friend asked, "Are you sure you're okay?"

"The CliffsNotes version: Donovan and I fell out, and I will be riding solo tonight at the party."

"You don't know. He may be at home now, ironing his tux," she said, trying to be positive.

I chuckled. "Doubt it."

"Well, call me when you get in."

"I will."

When I finally made it home, Donovan wasn't there, which was no shock to me. Over the past few weeks, his hours had been getting later and later. I'm sure that was by design because I was usually asleep by the time he made it in so that helped avoid an argument.

By the time I showered and slipped into my strapless, peach, silk gown, he still hadn't made it home.

I brushed my long locks up into a bun that I secured in place with a jeweled clip. I dug around in my jewelry box, and pulled out the diamond necklace Donovan bought me for my birthday a few years before, and slipped it on my neck.

A voice came from behind me. "You look beautiful."

I turned around; Donovan was standing in the doorway. His tie was loosened around his neck, his suit jacket draped over his arm.

"Are you coming?" I asked.

He undid the knot in his tie. "I'm tired," he said, sliding off his shoes and letting them hit the floor one at a time.

"So I have to go by myself?"

"Teri, I'm tired," he said, taking off his shirt. "Why don't you stay here with me?"

"You know I can't do that. I have to go represent the practice."

He sat on the bed for a second, staring at me. "Since when did you become the poster child for that practice? I'm sure a few other people will be there as well."

Before I could defend myself, he was in the bathroom, and I heard the shower come to life.

I checked my reflection in my mirror, and fought hard to hold back the tears that were threatening to mess up my makeup.

I called toward the closed bathroom door, and told my husband I was leaving.

I couldn't help but wonder if he was happy.

Chapter Three

I walked into the grand ballroom at the Ritz-Carlton, Atlanta, and was immediately overwhelmed by the beauty of the room. The warm glow from the sconce lighting and candles gave the giant ballroom the feel of a winter wonderland. There was soft music being pumped into a room that reeked of money, old and new. Our doctor's office was one of the sponsors of the fundraiser that benefited the Susan G. Komen for the Cure breast cancer fund. It was the only reason I didn't mind going every year. Patrons paid a huge price for dinner and drinks, then danced the night away. Donovan and I usually stayed through dinner, and then we would sneak upstairs to a room we had reserved in advance and have our own fundraiser. Not tonight.

I smiled and hugged my way through the crowded room, and bumped into Patty, one of the psychologists in the practice. She had avoided me like bad milk after the news of my promotion spread. I know it was eating her controlling behind up that I could possibly be her boss. She smiled, gave me a fake congratulatory hug, and told me she was happy for me. I just smiled and continued to work the room. I was relieved when I bumped into Harrison.

"Where is your husband?" he asked.

"He's at home. Not feeling well."

"And you came here? You need to be at home taking care of your man."

I smiled. "He's a big boy. He can measure NyQuil on his own."

Harrison's wife slid up to him and wrapped her arm around his waist. I tried to hide my shock at how tragically underdressed she was. Her navy blue two-piece maternity outfit looked like something better suited for a day of shopping at the mall than a black tie event. Her weave was tacky, and her makeup left a lot to be desired. I always believed that pregnant women were beautiful, that they had a special glow about them. Well, whoever coined that phrase obviously hadn't seen her. Next to Harrison's well-manicured appearance, she looked out of place. Even with all of that, I couldn't help but look at the swell of her belly and feel a twinge of jealousy.

She smiled. "Hello, Teresa."

"Hi, Michelle."

"I love your dress," she said as she ran her hand along my waist. "I remember when I was that small. Where is your fine-ass husband?"

"At home, nursing a cold. You know how they get when they feel sick; you'd think they weren't going to make it through the night."

She laughed and added her two cents by telling me about a time when Harrison had a virus, and she had to clean up behind him, and I do mean *behind* him. I smiled and excused myself while Harrison fussed at her for telling his business.

I walked by the buffet, eyeing the high-priced, low-taste food. I figured I could put in an hour, and then I was out. I would have more than enough time to make it home, cuss Donovan out, and still get a good night's sleep.

I spied the buffet table. Mangoes, watermelon, cantaloupe, and honeydew melons decorated the table alongside tiny sandwiches, meatballs, what looked like miniature quiche, and strawberries dipped in both dark and white chocolate. There was a carving station with roast beef and another meat that I couldn't make out. I picked up one of the small plates and began piling finger foods on it. I reached for a strawberry at the same time another hand did.

The man attached to that hand was gorgeous. His smile was infectious, and his Burberry cologne was like an aphrodisiac causing me to become aware of the heart between my legs.

"I'm sorry," he said. "You can go ahead."

"That's okay," I said, handing him the plastic tongs. "You go ahead. I don't need it anyway."

He took the plastic utensil from me, brushing his hand against mine, and causing the temperature in the room to shoot up about twenty degrees.

"You're Dr. McCall, right?"

I cut my eyes at him. "Right. Do I know you?"

His eyes sparkled as he talked. "You don't remember? We met last month at the medical conference at the Georgia World Congress Center."

I could barely remember what I'd done last week, so I lied, just to drag the conversation out, considering my only other option was Harrison and his chatty wife.

"Oh, yeah," I said. "I remember."

He raised an eyebrow then laughed. "No, you don't."

I chuckled. "You're right. I don't."

"That's okay. I don't mind introducing myself again."

I smiled and made my way toward my table as he followed.

I asked, "And you are?"

"Sean. Sean Morris," he said, flashing a beautiful smile.

I asked, "And what brings you to this lively party?"

"Uh, as a favor to a friend. He didn't want to come alone."

"Where is he?"

He looked around, frowned a little. "You know, I think I've been stood up, because I haven't seen him yet."

We laughed. I didn't want to, but I had to ask. "Um, is your friend your um . . . you know."

He leaned in and gave me a better look at his light brown eyes. "Is he my *boyfriend*?"

Just the way he said it, I knew he couldn't be gay. It didn't even sound right when he said it, but we got another good laugh at my expense.

"Are you married?" I asked.

He averted his eyes and said, "Divorced."

I took a sip of my coffee. "I'm sorry to hear that. I hope it wasn't messy."

"Aren't all divorces messy?"

With that, I thought about my own jacked-up marriage and quickly changed the subject. "What about a girlfriend?"

He chuckled. "I don't have a girlfriend."

"That's what they all say."

"I don't." He laughed.

I liked his laugh, and I definitely liked him.

We talked as we munched on our bland food and sipped coffee spiked with Kahlua.

He motioned to my wedding rings, and asked the question that would kill the mood for me.

"Where is Mr. McCall?"

I took a sip of my coffee. "At home."

"Really? He didn't want to play . . . dress-up, as you put it?"

I shook my head. "He's not the dress-up type."

"I see." He slid his hand across the table and touched mine, sending shockwaves through my body. "Did he see how good you looked before you left?"

My heart pounded so hard I thought it was going to jump out of my chest and run around on the table.

I lied, yet again. "He wasn't home. Why?"

19

"Because there is no way I would've let you leave looking like that, with or without me."

I pulled my hand away, and leaned back in my chair.

"You're sweet." I smiled.

"Just being honest. You look beautiful in that dress. Reminds me of Jennifer Lopez in that movie," he started. "The one where she's a maid."

I smiled. "Yes. I remember that movie. Cute movie."

He winked at me. "Cute doctor."

I checked my watch. "Listen, I'm having a great time, but I really need to go. I didn't realize how late it was."

"New friends will do that to you, make you lose track of things."

"Is that what you are? A new friend?"

"I can be."

There was something about the sound of his voice that was hypnotic. I attempted to relax and allow him to take me to a new level. Our conversation changed a thousand times as I allowed myself to completely get lost in what he was offering.

He told me that he was a cardiac surgeon at Crawford Long Hospital, handling pacemakers and angioplasty, but he was one of the on-call ER doctors for trauma.

He shared that, thanks to his divorce, he lived alone.

"She took everything?" I asked.

He took a sip of his Kahlua-laced coffee. "Just my heart."

"I'm sorry."

"Don't be. She cheated."

"Oh," I said, dropping my eyes to my half empty cup. "Sorry to hear that."

"Don't be." He smiled. "It was her loss."

Standing in front of the hotel waiting for the attendant to bring me my car, he asked me when he could see me again.

"You can't," I responded, looking out into the downtown traffic. Cars were bumper to bumper. Everyone was out trying to get their party on. I couldn't help but wonder if I was already dancing with the devil.

"Aww, come on now. Don't do this to me." He put his hand over his chest and made a sound like he was heartbroken, then flashed that smile again.

He was beautiful.

There weren't many men who could be pegged as beautiful, but he was one of them. His eyes sparkled in the lights of the awning; his smile was framed with dimples so deep I wanted to curl up in one and go to sleep. He reminded me of Allen Iverson, minus the braids and the bad attitude. I could tell the suit he was wearing was custom made for him by the way it framed his body.

"Why would I want to do that? I don't even know you. You could be a Ted Bundy, or worse—Jeffrey Dahmer in training, for all I know."

"I'm not a serial killer, and I definitely don't want to eat you. Well, not in that way." He gave me a smile. He reached in his jacket pocket and handed me one of his business cards.

I ignored his innuendo and looked down at the stark white card he'd just placed in my hand. "Dr. Morris, how do I know that?"

He crossed his heart with a manicured finger. "I give you my word."

The attendant pulled up and jumped out. He left my door open and my car running. The pimply-faced boy ran around the car and smiled, giving me my cue to give him his tip. I opened my LV bag and handed him a ten dollar bill.

"Look, I have to go."

"I enjoyed your company, doctor. I just want to sit down and talk, that's all. It's just coffee."

I had to admit, it felt good to flirt, and it felt even

better to be flirted with. If anything, it reminded me that I was still alive.

I smiled. "Can I think about it?"

He smiled. "I guess so, but I can't operate on my own heart if you break it."

"Okay." I laughed. He made me promise to call before he walked around and helped me get in the car.

He chuckled softly. "Bye, Miss Lady."

"My name is Teresa," I said before closing my door and pulling away.

It was damn near midnight when I got home. The only sound I could hear echoing through the huge house, other than my heels on the hardwood floor, was the television coming from the downstairs den. I could hear a newscaster, undoubtedly from CNN, commenting on Obama's healthcare reform.

I kicked my heels off at the front door, and headed toward the steps.

When I got downstairs, Donovan was sitting in his chair, remote in hand. I tossed my purse on the couch, and pulled the bun out of my hair, letting my hair fall down my back and across my shoulders. I looked up at the huge TV nestled on the wall. The story had switched from healthcare reform to the investigation into Michael Jackson's death.

I asked, "What's up?"

"Waiting up for you."

"Why? If you would've come, you wouldn't have had to wait up." I sank into the black leather couch.

"I told you I was tired."

"You know I hate going to those things by myself," I said.

"Well, you were in your element, so I don't know what the problem was."

He turned and looked at me. His eyes were glassy and red. My body became rigid, and I stood up.

"You're drunk," I said.

"No, I'm not."

22

I stood up and headed over to the small kitchenette nestled in the corner of the huge den.

He followed me.

I fumbled with the coffee pot as he asked, "What are you doing?"

"Making you some coffee. I am not trying to deal with you when you are like this."

He snatched the coffee strainer from my hand and tossed it into the sink. "I don't need coffee, Teri. I'm not drunk."

"I have to get up early, Donovan. I'm not in the mood for this."

He looked at me and shook his head. "You just don't get it, do you?"

I put my hands on my hips and leaned against the counter. "Get what?"

"You are like a ghost around here," he said, waving his hand toward the open kitchen. "I need a *wife*, Teresa, not some bigger than life, egotistical doctor who uses this half million dollar house like a rest stop."

That got my attention, mainly because he never called me Teresa. I had been Teri to him as long as I could remember. On so many levels, him calling me by my full name hurt; it desensitized our relationship.

"So what? You would rather me be here, cooking, and cleaning in this half million dollar house?" I snapped.

He ran his fingers through the dark curls on top of his head, stopping to scratch the crown. His five o'clock shadow had long since moved in, and he looked worn and tired.

He threw his hands up, looked in the direction of the steps that led to our bedroom, and started to walk away.

"If you aren't happy, Donovan, then why don't you just leave?"

He stopped in the archway, and with his back to me, he asked, "What did you just say?"

"What is the point of staying here if you aren't happy?" I said. "Leave."

My adrenaline was pumping overtime. I had never said that to him before, and judging from the change in his posture, if he had been drunk, he wasn't anymore.

He turned around. The Latin fire had been ignited in his eyes. "How are you going to tell me to leave MY house? I paid for this house! I'm the one who busted his ass to buy this overpriced brick box, because YOU wanted it! And now you want to tell me to leave? Fuck you, Teri. You get out!"

That hurt enough to almost make me back down, but it was too late. So I decided to throw some daggers of my own. "Damn, you're telling me to leave? She must've been really good for you to tell me to get out," I hissed.

He got up in my face, causing me to flinch and tense every muscle in my body. He started toward me, and got right in my face. The stench of alcohol came off of him, mixing with his cologne; the smell was nauseating. "Make that the last time you EVER tell me get out of MY house. If you don't like it here, YOU leave."

Just as fast as it had appeared, the fire died in his eyes, and he was on his way up the steps. I heard the door to the guest room slam closed. I swallowed hard a few times, tried to calm the storm in my stomach.

I looked down at my wedding ring . . . the three-carat stone became heavy . . . much too heavy for me to bear.

Chapter Four

"You look a mess, Teri."

I smiled at my friend and tossed a napkin across the table toward her. "I know. I need some sleep. This stupid offer for partner is killing me," I said, massaging my foot.

"No, it's not that. You look like you were up all night fighting and didn't win."

We were sitting on the patio of Fellini's on Ponce De Leon Avenue. Renee asked me to meet her for lunch. Traffic was crazy, with college students and wannabe college students all over the place. The sky was clear as a newborn's eyes; not a cloud in it.

I looked toward the parking lot where we parked our cars. It was closer to Dugan's, but I'm a pizza fanatic, and I wasn't in the mood for wings, so we walked up the block to Fellini's instead. The restaurant was packed to capacity, and I hoped nobody got stupid and put a dent in my car.

Renee asked, "So why didn't you call me when you got in last night?" She took a sip of her lemonade. "I mean, partner? That's a big deal!"

"Thanks." I smiled. It felt good to have her support.

My girl was wearing a pair of hip huggers that were so low, even Beyoncé wouldn't put her bodacious booty in them. She had on a short white T-shirt that had *BabyPhat* in glitter across the front, showing off her abs. Her hair was freshly twisted and rested on her shoulders. Her chocolate skin was fresh and free of cosmetics. She was naturally beautiful, and I admired that about her.

"Spill it." Renee got a serious tone about her. "What's up with you and your husband?"

I let out a sigh. "Marital bliss ain't all that's it's cracked up to be," I said, munching a slice of pizza.

"Why?"

"He's tired of the hours I am working, and now with this partner thing looming over my head . . . " I paused and thought about the way my life would change. "I don't know."

"Your marriage should come first, Teri."

"I know, Renee, but I enjoy what I do. I don't want to have to start a new career. Hell, I will be thirty-nine next year."

She didn't look convinced with my attempt at self-actualization. She shook her head and took a bite of her pizza.

"Y'all need to get it together," she said. "Tell your boss you can't do it."

"What! And risk never getting that offer again? Do you realize how much money I stand to make? The title and status alone." I shook my head. "I don't think so," I said, smoothing my ponytail.

"Sacrifice, Teri. Do you want your marriage to work?"

"I guess so."

"What do you mean *you guess so*? You've been married for over seven years; you need to figure it out."

I waved her off. "Yeah. Yeah, I do."

"Of course you do. That six figure salary is good, but it can't make your toes curl at two o'clock in the morning."

We both laughed. I almost told my friend about

26

my husband's anger—about the fire in his eyes. But I didn't.

She said, "And if you don't want him, I will take him."

"I don't think Derrick would appreciate that."

"Hey, he can live in the basement. Derrick would never know he was there!"

More laughter. Just what I needed. I missed hanging out with Renee. Ever since she got promoted, I hardly got to see her anymore. She worked a lot, but she loved her job. She lived and breathed accounting. She and her husband seemed to run their marriage like a factory. Everyone knew their job and did it without complaining—picking up kids, shopping, etc. To me they seemed to have it all figured out. They had date nights twice a month, even went on vacations together. I could tell they were made for each other, and deep down I envied that.

Renee, and I had been hanging strong since our days at West Fulton High, when she saved me from big, fat Aretha, who was trying to beat me up and take my lunch money in the cafeteria.

"So what are you going to do, Teri?"

"I don't know, *Mom*!"

"You can keep the sarcasm, because I don't want to hear it," she said.

"Whatever. What about your perfect marriage? Maybe you need to concentrate on that."

"Nope, 'cause when your marriage is perfect, like mine, you can counsel lost souls like yourself!" She laughed. I watched my friend's eyes light up as she laughed at her joke. I saw the peace and contentment that was in her life. I envied it and wanted to trade places with her, if only for a day.

Renee had one son, named Christopher, and she and Derrick were trying for another one. She was a month into trying. Life seemed to flow for her, while I was clawing, kicking, and screaming daily, trying to enjoy it. But for her, life seemed to just come up and lick her hand like a puppy in a pet store, looking for a home.

"How was your fundraiser?"

"It was"—I smiled at the memory—"interesting."

"What is that look about?"

"Nothing . . . what?"

She folded her arms across her chest. "Teri, I know you. What's his name?"

"There is none. I just realized last night that life is too short. I mean, think about it. One day, Michael Jackson is rehearsing for a tour, and the next day, he's gone."

"He must've been fine," she said, shaking her head.

"Fine as frog hair." I laughed.

I smiled as I thought about the conversation I had with Sean. He promised he was going to call me tonight around nine, and I was looking forward to it. I enjoyed our conversation, and was actually curious about him in more ways than one.

She leaned forward and wrinkled her nose. "Did you sleep with him, Teri?"

I laughed at her. "No I didn't, but I did have a nice conversation with a fine doctor. It was just what I needed."

"What you need to do is take your hot behind home and *talk* to your husband."

I tossed some money on the table for our waitress. "Let's go."

We got up and walked toward the parking lot. We stopped at her car. I smiled at the fact that her beat up old Honda was still hanging in there. It was at least ten years old, but she refused to buy another one. Her husband had told her many times to go and pick out something new—anything—but she said she liked not having a car payment.

"You really need to try to work it out with Donovan. And your doctor friend isn't the answer. No matter how fine he may be."

"You sound like Donovan. He's always talking about making it work or trying to work things out. But sometimes, I don't know what I want."

She smiled and winked. "Smart man."

"Oh, how's the new chick working out?" I asked, trying to divert the attention from my marriage. "The one that you hired last week."

"So far not so bad. She is shell shocked from a bad divorce, so she's a little quiet for my taste, but she seems cool enough. Has a son. I think she said he's four."

"Well, good. I hope she works out."

"Yeah, me too. She's the second person in this position in the last two months."

I looked at my watch. Donovan wanted me to meet him at his office today. I still couldn't believe he was working on a Saturday. How was that okay for him but not me?

"I mean it, Teri; I'm here for you. I still say you tell your boss thanks but no thanks." She checked her lipstick in the mirror on her car door.

I nodded and looked across the street at a group of college kids. They were young and stupid, with their whole lives in front of them. I just hoped someone in their lives cared enough to tell them that before they hit thirty.

"I gotta run," I said, hugging my friend.

"Call me later."

"I will."

I got to Donovan's office and rode the elevator to the fifth floor. My husband's watchdog secretary was on her post just outside his door, and she earned every dime he paid her. She was one hell of a call screener, and if you didn't have an appointment, you couldn't just waltz up asking to see anything but the elevator you just got off. I couldn't believe she actually came in on a Saturday to cater to him. I was almost jealous, considering I couldn't keep a secretary to save my life.

His secretary smiled when she saw me coming. She was an older white lady in her fifties, with light brown hair. Sue had been working for Donovan for years—ten to be exact. She was almost as overprotective of him as I was. We had her over a few times. You know, for holiday dinners, things like that, but I didn't know a whole lot about her other than she had a son who was in the Army and a husband who used to be.

"Good afternoon, Dr. McCall."

"Hi, Helen. Please call me Teri." I smiled. "Is Donovan in there?" I asked, pointing toward the huge wooden doors that led to his office.

"Yes, he is just finishing a conference call." She smiled up at me from behind her desk.

"Thank you."

I tapped lightly on the door before entering the massive office space. He was sitting behind his glass and chrome desk. A huge black and white picture of Martin Luther King Jr. adorned his wall; on the opposite wall was the same-sized picture of Malcolm X. My husband was always riding that line between good and just a little bit left of good. Doing the right thing, but not completely opposed to doing what needed to be done.

He was still on the phone, but I could tell from the tone of the conversation that it was close to ending. He motioned for me to close the door.

His office was spotless. The chrome flat screen monitor had colorful charts and spreadsheets on it. His glass top desk was covered with papers and folders. My attention went to his bookshelf. More specifically, to the spot where our wedding picture used to be. I blinked a few times and tried to make it appear. I scanned the office. It wasn't on his desk either. There was a picture from a golf trip he and Keith took the month before, even a picture of his mother. But no wedding picture.

"Teri."

His voice pulled me from my inventory session. Before he could say anything or get his story together, I asked him where our picture was.

"Where is it, Donovan?"

He pulled the picture from a desk drawer, minus the frame, and slid it across his desk to me. I smiled up at myself from the 8 x 10 glossy. I was dressed in white, glowing, and happy. That day, forever meant forever.

He said, "I smashed the frame one day when I was mad, and haven't gotten around to buying another one."

His smugness irritated me. I rolled my eyes and pushed the picture back to him.

"You owe me a picture frame. That frame was a wedding gift."

He just gave a nonchalant laugh and shook his head.

"Why did you want to see me?" I asked that question, and felt like a business associate, a client; someone he cared nothing about—not like a wife.

"I need to know what you want to do about our marriage." He pulled a folder out of his desk drawer and placed it on the desk in front of me.

It amazed me how our roles had switched. He was the victim now, the one who was hurt. The last six months, I was forced to push my hurt aside and pretend that Tracie didn't exist, because that was what he wanted. He apologized, and that was supposed to make it all better. All was supposed to be forgiven.

I flipped through the papers, not expecting to find what I did. I saw my name under the heading *Defendant*. His name resting under the heading of *Plaintiff*.

I read words like: *irreconcilable differences, uncontested*, and *division of assets* on the pages.

The words: *Divorce Decree* sliced through me, cutting me deep.

I wanted to know when he had them drawn up, but couldn't seem to form the words. Part of me wanted to rip them to shreds and toss them in his face, but my hands were shaking so badly, I couldn't.

"What is this, Donovan?"

"It's an ultimatum."

I cut my eyes at him. "Excuse you?"

"It's either our marriage or that job."

I blinked against tears and swallowed. I tried to read the papers, but my vision was cloudy. He stood to his feet and moved around the huge desk that was separating us.

I braced myself and waited for the bell to ring, signaling the beginning of our twelve rounds.

I exploded. "I can't believe you! When did you do this?"

"Last month."

"*Last month!*" My voice hit an octave that would've made Mariah Carey jealous. "You have to be kidding me."

"Let's not pretend," he started. "Our marriage is a mess."

"Is that right?" I asked, taking on a defensive tone. "Why is that? Is it because you couldn't manage to keep your dick in your pants?"

He closed his eyes. My question hit like a right hook that he wasn't expecting; it staggered him.

"By sleeping with that trick, you started this, not my job!"

He turned his back to me, walked toward his bookcase. "I'm not going there with you. I've already told you how that went down."

"What—the fuck—ever."

"If you're not gonna let it go so we can move on, then we're wasting our time and this marriage is over, Teri."

"Apparently so! You filing for divorce behind my back!"

"The understood doesn't need to be explained."

"Bullshit!" I screamed at him. "That's all the explanation you got? You were lonely? Then you should have *bought* a bitch! Not slept with one!"

"I wasn't getting what I needed at home, Teri! You were never there. If it wasn't work, it was Renee, or some event for the practice."

"Since day one of our marriage I've given a hundred percent!"

"Are you saying I haven't?"

"No, I'm saying that I decided to start making my own mark, and you throw a temper tantrum like a little kid by cheating! Not a good look, Donovan!"

I shook my head against the memory of the day UPS ruined my life.

Six months ago, a cardboard box, sent anonymously, held everything I had managed to ignore over the previous year. Love letters full of promises, ticket stubs to Florida. Keepsakes from dinners, and hotels, all charged to his Visa. Everything charged over the course of a year. Everything mailed to me with a note telling me I could have my husband back, and dumb-ass me never even realized he had been taken.

I remembered the fight we had, the weeks I spent with Renee, and all the tears and promises made to get me to come back home. It all came flooding back, threatening to drown me where I stood.

"You did this to us. You put this wedge between us," I snapped.

"No, I didn't." He shook his head. "Damn it, Teri, I am not going to let you put all of this on me."

"When you made the decision to sleep with Tracie, you took all of this on your head."

He shook his head and continued to deny that it was his fault. "Your work hours are unrealistic when you're married. You love your job more than you do me."

I threw my hands up. "You can't be serious! You know how much I love my job! And because you are *jealous* you want me to walk away."

That upset him he shifted, his eyes changed from intense to angry right before my own.

He shouted. "You just don't get it, do you?"

I waved the divorce papers in his face. "This is your idea of working it out, talking about it?"

"I am trying to get your attention, Teri! Ever since—" He stopped, refused to speak the memory, and blew out a breath. "You have been distant for a long time."

"Say it, Donovan! You blame me anyway, so say it!" I screamed. "Say it! Ever since I miscarried!"

He walked over to the window, looked at the rest of the world going about their day, and then back to me. His face said what his heart wouldn't let him.

I said, "You blame my job, don't you?"

His posture changed enough to let me know I have hit a nerve.

"Answer me, Donovan!"

"Teri, the doctor said—"

"I know what the damn doctor said, Donovan. I was there!"

Over two years ago, Dr. Burton had said words like: *stress*, *incompetent cervix*, and *pre-term labor*. Things that could've contributed to the miscarriage, but nothing helped us to understand why it happened, or why I hadn't been able to conceive since.

When my contractions started, I was in the middle of a counseling session. I managed to ignore them so I could finish, and start on my notes after the session. The phone rang while I was doing my dictation, and when I picked it up, my husband asked how I was doing. He was so excited about the baby that I had to tell him to limit his calls to three times a day in order for me to get any work done. He always told me he wanted a big family. But being that I had just started with the practice, and I had developed a good relationship with everyone, one child was too much for me at the time, and unfortunately, my actions reflected that.

I told him about the pains and he told me to go to the hospital, but I really wanted to finish my notes so I could have them on Dr. Lee's desk first thing in the morning. I told him I probably just needed to increase my water. He reluctantly agreed, but made me promise to call him when I was on my way home.

An hour was too late. I ended up in the back of an ambulance with a paramedic delivering my twenty-week- old baby. Twenty-eight weeks is considered viable.

A life. Maybe not a perfect, illness-free life, but alive nonetheless.

Donovan made it just in time to hold her and cry with me before they took both of us to the hospital. At that point, I just wanted to go home and die.

We lost our daughter that day, along with a huge chunk of our marriage. Our foundation had been cracked; making it easy for his affair to seep in, causing further damage.

As far as the miscarriage, my doctor blamed the unknown. Donovan blamed my job, my long hours, my lack of sleep, and disregard for taking care of myself. I wasn't sure who to blame, so I internalized my hurt and anger and on occasion blamed myself as well.

"Teri, you are making this too damn hard."

"Me!" I tossed the divorce papers in his direction. They bounced off his chest, and one by one, floated to the floor.

He stood his ground. "Yes, you!"

That made me angrier, and I went off. Donovan tried to take his place in this dog fight by exploding, but him trying to out-yell me was pissing me off even more. Our fight shook the walls of his office. I knew his secretary could hear, but I didn't care. I reminded him

35

of the trips he had taken with her, the dinners, and the hotel rooms. I let him know how our memories of Florida were now stained with visions of him and her there. That piece of history slowed his roll.

My tears flowed. I was exhausted, and I could tell he was too.

I bent down and snatched the divorce papers off the floor, and stormed out, leaving him alone.

Just as alone as I felt.

Chapter Five

Donovan didn't even come after me.

I couldn't drive home fast enough. I ran past his secretary so fast, the papers on her desk fluttered in my wake.

I sped through downtown like a woman possessed. I rode past the bank where I met my husband. That memory came back to me, and calmed me.

I was making a deposit at SunTrust, where he was the branch manager. He promised me high yields on my money if I opened up an investment account. He was dressed in a black Armani suit; his build led me to believe he was a former ball player. His eyes were so hypnotic. I couldn't resist his lunch invitation.

With his lunch invitation, I found out that his mother was from Cuba, and his father, an African-American, was from Atlanta. They met while his father was in the military, and Donavan was the beautiful result. His mother died of cancer, and his father, not long after, died from a broken heart. It wasn't long before his dinner invitation turned into late nights, which turned into later nights, and earlier mornings.

I was fresh off of receiving my doctorate, working at a doctor's office in downtown Atlanta when he proposed. His career was sky-rocketing, and he rode that ride all the way to a jewelry store and picked out a three carat, G-quality, princess cut diamond. Flawless.

I remember sitting at my desk, receiving flower after flower. Not *flowers* but flower. He had a dozen red roses sent to me—one at a time. By the time the eleventh rose made it to my desk, everyone was coming around to my desk trying to figure out what was going on. I was on the phone with Renee, my excitement oozing out of my pores.

"Has he called you yet?" she asked, popping her gum in my ear.

"No, and why are you chewing that gum like you are scared someone is going to take it out of your mouth?"

She laughed. "My bad."

The second line on my phone rang, and the caller ID said FRONT DESK. My heart jumped in my chest.

"Renee, I have to go."

"No, wait! Is it him, is he there?"

I hung up and tried to suppress my excitement. The receptionist sounded like she had just had an encounter with Don Juan himself as she told me I had a visitor.

In the lobby, my future husband was standing there holding a single rose the last to complete my dozen. He was also holding a little black ring box.

Happy times.

Times I thought would never end.

But now, our trips to Florida had been marred with visions of him and her. Weekends when we had holed up in a hotel downtown, sweating and panting, were replaced with thoughts of them having sex. She knew I existed, and became a part of my life without asking. I didn't have the option of a third person joining me in bed. They had shared fluids; so to me, it was like I had slept with her.

To this day, I never knew what she looked or sounded like, but to me, she was every woman I passed: short, tall, fat, skinny, black or white. Donovan was very careful that our worlds never collided.

Two hours later, as I tossed a load of clothes in the machine, my cell phone rang. It was Renee.

"Have you worked things out yet?"

It had been two days since we had our argument, and we were barely speaking. I told her about the blow up, and how he had shoved divorce papers in my face. My voice cracked when I told her I was sick and tired of him and his ultimatums.

"Why don't you come and stay with Derrick and me?"

"I am not leaving my house because he slept with that trick!"

"Teri—"

"Uh-uh. Not gonna happen."

"Why are you torturing yourself?" Her line clicked, but she didn't answer.

"I am not torturing myself."

"Just be careful."

I sighed. "I'll be fine."

"What about counseling?"

"Don't think he would go."

"Church?"

"I know he wouldn't go."

"Oh! Y'all should come visit my church," she said, ignoring what I just told her.

She had talked so many times about us visiting her church. I had watched their bishop on television before.

"Who is that, Dale Bronner, right?"

"Yup. I think you guys would enjoy it."

I knew I would, but Donovan had never been very religious. We had attended a few churches in the neighborhood. You know, Christmas time, Easter, the obligatory holidays. The times of the year most people think are good enough to go and repent for the dirt of the rest of the year.

I knew better though. I was raised in church—

Trinity AME. Zion. The small white church right across the street from my grandmother's house in Pittsburgh, Pennsylvania. Rain, sleet or snow—she shuffled us out that front door, and across the street. I remembered Sunday school lessons, and Vacation Bible School during the summer.

My friend continued. "Just think about it."

"Renee, I don't know what to do. I love my husband, but this is becoming too much. Can you believe he wants me to quit?"

She let out a chuckle. "Girl, if Derrick made as much as your man did, I would be at home, scratching my behind all day if that's what he wanted me to do."

"You know that's not me."

"What about dancing?"

I let a groan escape my throat as my mind traveled back to times of toe shoes and dance classes. I really thought I was going to be the next diva ballerina. But when you are young, and no one seems to want to be your cheerleader and see your vision like you do, you just follow the crowd.

"I'm too old."

"No, you're not, and you are in great shape. Well, except for that big ole booty!"

I laughed. "Shut up. Especially, since we wear the same size jeans."

She couldn't help but laugh. "Yeah, and I know I'm fine."

Our conversation changed direction fifty times. From how she wanted to cut her hair to how I needed to buy a new microwave to Mike Vick getting out of jail, but it always came back to the same subject—my screwed up marriage.

It was my turn for my line to beep. I looked at the caller ID, and it said UNKNOWN CALLER, but I decided to take it anyway.

After saying hello twice with no response, I hung up.

"Who was that?"

"They hung up. Guess they didn't want to talk to me."

"Probably because they know you got a big ass!" She laughed at her attempt to make fun of me.

I laughed. "Look, I gotta go. My big ass needs to be washed."

"Yeah, I need to get ready for work tomorrow," she said.

"Call me later."

I started gathering clothes for the washing machine when I heard my cell phone vibrating against the inside of my purse. I looked at the clock and remembered that Sean had left me a message the night before saying he was going to call. I answered it with hopes of good conversation and an escape from my stressful world.

"Hi."

"Hello, Miss Lady."

The bass in his voice relaxed my body like warm bath water.

"I didn't think you were going to call."

"I told you I would."

"Now, explain to me again what it is you want from me."

I sank down on the couch and listened to his voice, all while imagining what he was doing on the other end of the line.

He started to try to convince me to meet him, and that's when I stopped him.

"You know that I can't do that."

"Why?"

"I'm married, remember?"

"So? Married women eat, don't they?"

I laughed. "Whatever. Look, call me later in the week. Maybe we can work something out."

"Okay. I'm gonna hold you to that."

I smiled. "You do that."

We hung up, and I flipped channels and sipped a glass of wine, willing it to soothe my nerves. Before I realized it, afternoon turned into late evening. The clock told me that my husband's late work day was turning into a late night at work.

Another glass of wine went down.

I couldn't help but remember how happy we used to be. We would stay up at night sometimes, laughing and talking about nothing. We would take spur of the moment trips to Florida for the weekend and never leave the room. Now his long hours and short temper were a serious stress point for our marriage.

I paced the den, trying to let the Zinfandel do its job, and relax me, but my anger fought it every step of the way, keeping me tense and on edge.

After an hour of clock watching, the sandman came and slammed me on the couch, and forced me into a restless sleep.

My aching head and full bladder woke me up.

It was after ten when I got up to use the bathroom in the hall, before going to the kitchen to look out the window to see if Donovan's E-Class Mercedes was resting in its spot in the driveway.

It wasn't. My car slept alone.

My mouth was dry. Alcohol will do that to you. I gulped down a half bottle of water before climbing the steps to my room. I wanted to take a bath, but didn't want to wait for the huge Jacuzzi tub to fill up, so I settled for a shower. With the door closed, I got the water so hot the bathroom quickly filled up with steam.

I stripped, and turned the dimmer light down. I still felt a little buzzed, and the water felt good on my skin. I let it run over my head and through my hair. I admired my legs as I washed them. They were still pretty tight from my dancing days; a good pair of heels still made my calves pop like they should.

My shape hadn't changed much either. I was five

feet, four inches, and a size 8. I had put on a few pounds with my pregnancy, but I managed to Slim-Fast them off in no time. I was fit, but shapely. I got my big behind from my father's side of the family, and my speedy metabolism from my mother's. It seemed I was the only thing they managed to get right.

I allowed my tension to float above me in the lavender-scented steam, and let my frustrations wash down the drain with the soap suds. An hour later, I was stretched across the bed in one of Donovan's Morehouse T-shirts and a pair of panties, flipping channels when I heard the alarm on the house chirp, letting me know that Donovan had finally made it home.

I heard Donovan's voice calling from the kitchen. "Teri!"

I checked the clock again. It was almost midnight. I wasn't sure how to feel. I eyed my purse, which held the divorce papers.

Throughout the night, I thought about signing them so many times, but I wasn't sure I was ready for lawyers and judges to decide how the rest of my life would be spent.

Alimony.
No alimony.
I get the house.
He gets the dog.
I'm sorry, Your Honor, we don't have a dog.
Well, ma'am, you need to buy one and give it to him.

Donovan made his way upstairs. I could hear the change jingling in his pockets. His footsteps were heavy as he came in the room and stood at the foot of the bed.

"Where have you been?" I asked.

He looked at me like I was crazy. "What are you talking about? I was at work."

"Until midnight, Donovan?" My words were sharp.

"I called you and left you two messages. I told you I was still at work, and then called again to tell you I was meeting Keith for a beer."

"I didn't hear the phone ring."

"I called," he said while peeling off his clothes and tossing his shirt in the hamper.

I shook my head and started scrolling through the caller ID.

My mind was replaying tonight trying to remember if the phone had rung. "I don't know what you are talking about, Donovan."

"I don't know what to tell you. I called." His voice began to rise. I stood to my feet, got ready to fight and defend what I thought was right.

He turned and headed down the hall. I tossed my phone on the bed and was on his heels, trying to get him to explain the lost hours of the night.

He stopped on a dime and did a 180-degree turn right there in front of me. Now my husband was facing me in the dim track lighting of the hallway.

"I'm tired, Teri."

"Where have you been all night?"

"I went out for drinks—that's it! Nothing more. Why are you trying to make something out of nothing?"

"And you couldn't call me and let me know where you were?"

He ran his hand over his hair. "I am not doing this right now."

"Why the hell not! You were with her, weren't you?"

His tone rose, the flames in his eyes began to rise, and his Latino accent began to blend with his perfect English. He threw up his hands and asked me, "Have you signed the divorce papers?"

"Excuse you?"

"You heard me! I am sick of this shit, Teri. Did you sign the damn papers? I'm through with defending myself to you."

That stopped me in my tracks and made me back-pedal.

"I don't want to do this, not now." I turned to walk

away and he grabbed me, flung me around, and in the next moment his hand was around my throat.

"No! We're going to do this *now*. You started this; now finish it!"

In that moment, I hated him. I hated Tracie, and I hated Dr. Lee. I fought. Kicked. I tried to pry his fingers loose, but he wouldn't let up. His grip tightened as he bit his bottom lip.

"Donovan!"

My scream was weakened by the pressure from his hand around my throat. I tried to get away, but he threw me on the floor. He pinned me down and forced my legs open, tearing my panties off while undoing his pants.

I cried and screamed at him, begging him not to.

The fire coming from him was intense, taking over his whole demeanor, threatening to burn our house down. In the dimly lit hall, he came across as scary, evil.

He continued to try to force himself inside of me, but I wasn't open or wet enough, and it was painful. Tears fell from my eyes and down the sides of my face.

Suddenly, his face softened, and then he stopped. A look of shame came over him as sobs threatened to take over my body as my chest rose and fell.

"I—I'm sorry," he stammered, rolling away from me.

At that point, I lost control and lunged at him. I positioned myself on top of him. A look of panic and confusion spread across his face.

"Teri, what are you doing? Get off of me."

My hand found his semi-hard penis, and I began manipulating it. I squeezed and rubbed him, never taking my teary eyes from his. I wanted him to love me the way he used to, before everything got so screwed up. Our anger filled the air above us; the hurt was still in me, but it was different. He was my medicine, my salve that could make it all better.

His breathing slowed down as he jerked with the movement of my hand.

I brought him to me, and led him into what was now a warm, wet place. The place where he belonged. He closed his eyes as I took him in; and in that moment, we were one. The way it was supposed to be.

Heat rose deep inside, making me weak. I moved my hips slow at first, then a little faster. I ran my hand along his face and made him open his eyes to look at me.

"Tell me you love me," I whispered.

Through staggered breathing, he did as he was told. "I love you, Teri."

His hands moved to my hips, grinding me into him and helping me match his rhythm. The sweat running down my body mixed with our love.

Both of us were hotter than Atlanta in the middle of July.

I moved my hips in deep circles. His hips rose off the carpet to meet me. The rug burned my knees, but I didn't care. As I felt my orgasm rising, my legs began to tremble. An animalistic growl escaped my husband's lips, letting me know he was close. I wanted us to end this ride together. I reached down and led his thumb to the spot that would make that happen. Fire spread through me as he played with my little bundle of nerves. My breathing changed from ragged to harsh, matching my husband's fevered pattern. I became light-headed as he pumped fast and hard, trying to force out all his pain and anguish while I did the same. We both came hard and loud as our moans and grunts filled the empty house, turning our house into a home for the first time in months.

Chapter Six

It was almost eleven before I dragged my butt out of bed and began my Monday.

Donovan was dressed, and out the door before I could roll over twice. I didn't have any patients until the afternoon which was a good thing. I always planned my Monday that way, just in case I had a good weekend. My phone rang as I was making my first cup of coffee.

"Hello."

"Dr. McCall, this is Eva. I was wondering if you were going to be in the office today."

She had been asking if I would help her make up her class schedule. I tried hard to help her out. It was obvious that she was educationally challenged, but with three kids, a receptionist's salary just wasn't enough. So I told her to go back to school and get a degree.

"My first appointment isn't until one, and I didn't plan on coming in before then."

Then I thought about it. I did have some work that I needed to catch up on. I figured I could help out the helpless, and finish up my work—Kill two birds with one stone.

"You know what, Eva," I said. "I'll be there in an hour."

I took a quick shower, picked out a nice knee-length, orange-and-brown skirt with a matching top, and pulled out my chocolate brown boots. I loved this time of year; boots, and coats were my weakness. I smoothed my hair back into a shiny ponytail then went downstairs to my office to check my e-mails before I left.

My inbox was full of a lot of offers for increased sex drive, money in my checking account by tomorrow, and hot, hot, barely legal girls.

Delete.

Delete.

Delete.

I looked around what was supposed to be my office. Donovan had done a lot of the remodeling himself, and it was coming together nicely. My huge bookcase was due to be delivered along with the artwork I ordered. I smiled at the memory of last night, at the possibility of what working from home could mean for my marriage.

I dialed Renee on my way to the office. I dialed all of her numbers until I caught her at her office.

She asked, "How was your weekend?"

"It was okay, no arguments."

"I told you. Y'all needed to come to church with me yesterday."

I groaned. "Don't start with that again."

"You have to acknowledge Him, Teri. He wants to make this better."

"So you are telling me that He is allowing us to go through this?"

"He is waiting for you to give your marriage over to Him, so he can fix it."

I shook my head. I didn't want her to start preaching to me, but she did. She went on and on about tithing, marriage seminars, and retreats; tools that the church offers to strengthen and solidify a marriage, all ways that God wants to help us help ourselves.

"I'll talk to Donovan and I'll let you know."

"Don't wait too long."

"I won't."

"All right, bye."

I made my way through the office. It was pretty

dead for a Monday. I finger-waved to Harrison as I walked past his office. I could tell he was trying to get my attention, so I sped up. I stopped and checked my mailbox that was full of messages. There were messages from people wanting appointments, needing to change appointments, and good old Mr. Wendell and his clowns.

When I got to my office, I found Eva sitting at her desk typing away on the computer. Her small frame was covered in a dress that was way too big for her. Her hair was pulled back in a ponytail like mine, but her hair was store bought; mine was inherited. She didn't have on any makeup, making her appear much younger than her twenty-five years. Her caramel complexion was flawless. Her dark brown eyes lit up when she saw me.

She smiled and stood up, following me into my office.

"Hi, Eva."

"Hi, Dr. McCall. I thought you had changed your mind."

"I left the house a little late," I said, flipping through a stack of papers on my desk. "Eva, please call me Teri."

She just smiled and nodded. I tried to speed the meeting up. I still hadn't talked to Donovan about last night, and I wanted to track him down as soon as I could.

"You want some coffee before we get started?" I asked.

She shook her head, picked up a notepad, and handed it to me. She had course numbers and descriptions scribbled on the yellow paper. Everything seemed to be in order, so I still wasn't sure what she needed me for.

"Are you trying to take all of this next semester?" I asked.

She smiled. "I was gonna try. It would be considered a full load."

"Wow. I'm impressed. Well, let's get started."

We went over her schedule, and I helped her pick

out her core classes while I sifted through my own work. When we were finished, I jotted down my e-mail address for her to keep in touch outside of work, just in case she hit a snag in one of her classes.

"Thank you!" she said, staring at the paper as if she had just gotten an autograph.

After chatting with her and checking the news on CNN.com, I tried to catch up on my files.

The sessions that I had that day kept my mind off of my own problems. My first appointment began with a woman who'd lost her husband over in Iraq. She had recently given birth, so she was dealing with that on top of postpartum depression. She was harboring some abandonment issues, and was unloading them on her newborn as well.

I took about thirty minutes to scarf down half a sandwich and a diet Coke before my second patient of the afternoon came. She was a mother of three who suffered from bipolar disorder and mild depression. My third patient of the day was Mr. Wendell. I tried to concentrate as he tried to rationalize his fear of clowns: the oversized shoes, big hair, white makeup. "What are they trying to hide?" he would ask.

Toward the end of the day, I was sitting at my desk waiting for my last appointment when the phone rang. I picked up, hoping it wasn't Dr. Lee. I had yet to give him an answer on the partnership.

I breathed a sigh of relief when I discovered it was Sean. "Hello, Mr. Morris. How are you?"

"I want to see you. Meet me for dinner." His voice was intense, to the point.

"I can't, Sean. And besides, what do you mean you miss me? You don't even know me."

"I'm trying to get to know you. Just have drinks with me."

I smoothed back my ponytail, sucked in some air, and then blew it out. "I don't know."

"It's just food, Teresa."

I shocked myself when I told him to call me Teri.

"Okay," he said. "Teri. It's just food, dinner. That's all. Two colleagues talking over dinner."

"I don't—"

"Come on, Teri. I promise I'll be good," he said.

I ran my tongue over my teeth, letting the offer roll around in my head and crash into every voice telling me to tell him no.

"Let me think about it. And I'll call you back."

"Okay. Okay. You promise?"

I couldn't help but smile. "Yes, I promise."

I hung up and tried Donovan's cell, and got his voicemail, so I dialed his work number. He answered on the first ring.

My voice echoed. "Take me off speaker phone."

He picked up the receiver. "Where are you?"

"In my office."

He was quiet. I heard paper rustle and voices fade in and out before he returned to the conversation.

"I am in the middle of something. Can I call you back?"

His shortness got under my skin in the worst way. It was as if the other night never happened. I wanted to tell him that when I picked up my cell phone the next morning, I did see his missed calls from the previous night. Instead, I told him that I was going to meet Renee for dinner after work and I would be late getting home. Things were back to normal quicker than a supermodel's waistline after giving birth, and it bugged me. I wanted him to give me a reason to tell Sean no—any reason—but instead, I got confirmation.

"Yeah . . . . okay," he said.

"Whatever, Donovan. Bye."

I hung up before he had a chance to irritate me any further.

I heard a tap on the door. I stood up, smoothed the front of my suit, and slapped a smile on my face. She was my last appointment of the day. I just needed to get through one more hour and I was free.

The woman that walked in was beautiful. Her skin was flawless, her hair cut was precise, and her suit was expensive. She smiled and extended her hand for me to shake. I introduced myself as she took a seat on my leather couch.

"You must be Monica Duquesne," I said, picking up my notebook and taking my seat in the chair across from her.

"Yes, I am. Nice to meet you."

"So, Monica, what brings you to me today?"

Her voice was sultry, silky. "I've been experiencing depression. I can't seem to shake it. My primary care doctor suggested that maybe I come see you."

For the next hour, I took notes, and I listened to her weave me the tale of a lonely, scorned lover. I felt my body tense as her story became my own.

Every so often, her eyes would lose their sparkle, like someone had turned her off, but just as fast, she would rebound. My humanity wanted to reach out to her, but I knew as her therapist that was something I shouldn't do. She came across as very needy, which probably led her to a married man. She told me about a pregnancy that wasn't meant to be, and how he got her through that, but not long after, he left her. She told me she had no other relatives in Atlanta, and was dealing with all of this by herself.

Hearing her story softened me to her, and made her more human, not as annoying. I felt sorry for her. Sorry for her lost pregnancy, which I could relate to, and sympathize with.

"Why would you want him after all he did to you?"

She spoke barely above a whisper. "I love him."

"Do you think that this is really the best situation for you?" I asked her.

She shook her head, but didn't speak.

"You're correct; it doesn't sound like that relationship was very healthy for you."

She didn't answer me. She just stared at me, letting her eyes answer for her.

I continued. "Do you think he loves you?"

She nodded.

"How do you know that?"

"He told me."

That couldn't help but make me wonder what promises and lies Donovan had fed to Tracie. Did he make her feel the way this woman felt? Did he tell her that he loved her too?

The small clock chimed, letting me know that her hour was up. I stood up and flipped through my organizer. I found my next available date and filled out an appointment card, and handed it to her.

"I would like to recommend meeting once a week for now." I smiled at her. "You seem like a strong, beautiful woman with an even stronger mind. We'll work through this."

"Thank you." Her voice was barely above a whisper.

"You're welcome. My number is on the back if you need me before then."

She looked at the card then to me. "I'll keep that in mind."

After she left, I started putting my notes on tape so I could get ready to leave.

"You are still here?" Eva's voice came from behind me.

I looked at my watch, then at her. "Yeah, I am just waiting for my husband to get off work. Why are you still here?"

"Was doing a little studying, and I don't have to pick my son up from my mom's for another hour."

She took a seat in the chair across from me. "What does your husband do?"

"He's a—he's an investment banker," I said, scratching my temple. I was very distracted and was definitely ready to get the heck out of there.

"Wow," she said, sounding interested. "That sounds interesting."

I wrinkled up my nose. "Not really, just a bunch of number crunching."

I pretended I was looking for something, and hoped she would take my subtle hint and leave, but she didn't.

She asked, "You wanna get something to eat? There's a Ruby Tuesday down the street."

"You know, I would like to, but I am really trying to get out of here. I have to meet my husband at home," I said, trying not to sound too harsh.

"Okay," she said. "Oh, you have another message from that Darienne lady."

I tried to remember what I did with her number.

"I'll call her before I leave. I am going to finish up here and then head out." I grabbed a file off my desk and headed to the copy machine.

"Maybe next time." I called back to her as I headed down the hall.

Just as I got to the copier, my cell phone rang. RESTRICTED came across the small screen. Against my better judgment, I hit the button and answered.

"Hello."

"Dr. McCall?"

That question bothered me, mainly because the call was coming through on my private cell phone, not my work cell. Everyone that called my personal cell knew who they were calling, and none of them called me Dr. McCall.

"Yes."

Click!

Chapter Seven

When Eva finally left the office, I called Sean and told him I would meet him after all.

I called Renee and let her know what I was planning to do, as well as to set up my alibi. Of course, once she heard what I was gonna do, she freaked.

"What are you thinking? Donovan is gonna kill you."

"First of all, he's not gonna find out, and second of all, what harm can it do? We are meeting in a public place. Lots of people, no pressure."

She sighed, letting me know she didn't approve. I heard papers shuffling. She must've brought work home.

"I don't believe you," she finally said.

"Oh, shut up! It's not the end of the world. It's just dinner."

"I don't know what you are trying to prove."

"I am not trying to prove anything."

"What about him?" she asked. "How do you think Donovan feels?"

"Excuse you?" Now I was getting mad.

She continued, ignoring my growing attitude. "Both of you are being selfish, and putting your own feelings and wants first. That does *not* make a marriage."

My friend started to get psychological on me. Taking on my role, she expressed the good sense that I offered up to my clients but couldn't seem to secure for myself. She told me that she felt my husband and I were playing an emotional tug-of-war; neither of us wanting to let go first, and both of us were throwing hurt and pain in each other's faces. She said that neither of us wanted to admit nor accept fault, and reminded me that this was not what God wanted for us.

"So you think Sean is the answer?" she asked.

"I don't know what the answer is. Maybe I would feel better if I cheated, but dinner is not cheating, Renee."

"That's stupid, Teri. You're not a teenager; you know exactly what you're doing."

I didn't say anything. I wanted her to be on my side, but she wasn't taking sides in this. She wasn't betraying our friendship, but instead, being a friend to us both. Just like she'd been since she stood next to me on my wedding day, when I pledged to love him forever and he did the same.

"Fair is fair," I said.

I heard her suck her teeth. "And stupid is as stupid does."

"Who are you now? Forrest Gump? Are you trying to tell me you've never thought about it?"

"No."

"You're lying."

She laughed. "Whatever. No, I haven't. Plus, Denzel is married."

"And if he wasn't, he wouldn't want your rusty butt."

We both laughed.

"Don't do anything stupid, Teri. Donovan is trying."

"Yeah, trying to get on my damn nerves."

"He made a mistake. Either let it go or let him move on. You can't make any progress walking backwards."

"Who died and made you a guru?"

Renee continued, "Trust me. It ain't worth it. Teri, you are looking in the wrong spot. Talk to your husband. Something is wrong on both ends. He stepped out, and now you're talking about doing the same." She added, "Nothing good can come out of you sleeping with another man."

Again, I didn't say anything. I knew she was right, but I didn't want her to be. There was a huge hole in my heart, kicked there by my husband. I was hurting, and nobody seemed to understand.

"I gotta go, Renee. I'll call you later."

She hung up on me. I could tell she was pissed, but at this point, it seemed like no one cared about me being mad, hurt, or depressed. So why should I care?

An hour later, I walked into Sambuca's on weak knees. I was so nervous about meeting Sean that I could've peed my pants. I changed clothes twice, and redid my hair three times. I decided to leave my hair down and dress in all black. I thought it made me appear more mysterious. Why, I don't know, but it seemed like a good idea at the time.

The white on white of the dining room was elegant. The linens on the tables were topped with white lilies, and candles in sconces were the only lighting in the windowless room. The flickering of the light gave the room a very relaxing and romantic glow. The room was buzzing with friends and lovers. People were laughing and making plans for later, while couples huddled in corners.

I noticed Sean sitting at the bar. He was wearing what appeared to be a dark Armani suit, and was sipping on a drink. I started in his direction when he looked up. His diamond studs sparkled in the dim lighting. He smiled and stood up when he saw me.

"I'm glad you came," he said, hugging me and planting a small kiss on my cheek. "I thought you were going to stand me up."

All I could do was smile and try to ignore the voice in my head telling me to go home. A short, white female in a black and white hostess uniform came and whispered something in his ear. Sean took my hand as she led us to the back of the quaint restaurant. The smell of food floated around the room, causing my stomach to rumble.

We took our place at the round table, and he ordered a bottle of red wine.

"You're beautiful, you know that?"

I took a sip of the glass of water sitting in front of me. "Thank you, but you don't have to compliment me. I'm already here."

He laughed. "I know. I thought I was going to have to kidnap you."

Our eyes met, and for a brief moment I thought he was serious.

The hostess came back and placed the bucket next to the table. My stomach was in so many knots that I didn't think my food would digest, so I ordered a salad.

"You don't have to be cute. You can get real food. I think I have a twenty in my wallet." He laughed.

"That's good to know." I smiled.

After our waitress left, I searched his face, trying to find any hint of craziness.

He laughed. "What? Do I have something hanging out of my nose?"

"No. Just trying to figure out what I am doing here."

He took a sip of his wine and smiled. "To get to know me better, right?"

"If you say so."

I put my glass to my lips and tasted the sweet liquid.

He said, "So tell me about your marriage."

I shook my head. "Oh, no . . . you don't want to hear about that."

"Yes, I do."

I gave him a half smile. "We're just like any other couple. We have our issues, but we're working through them."

"Do you think your marriage will last?"

I held up my hand. "Okay, I really don't want to go there. I want to enjoy tonight. Is that okay?"

He nodded slowly. "You're right. I apologize."

Eventually, I managed to put Donovan out of my mind during dinner. Sean and I laughed, and somehow convinced ourselves that what we were doing was okay, and that we weren't opening up Pandora's box knowing we both would never be able to close it again.

Sean's smile was contagious, and it made me conjure up one of my own. Every time I thought about coming up with a bogus excuse to leave, his smile convinced me to stay.

I asked, "Where do you live again?"

"Why? Are you coming over?"

I coughed, and almost choked on the salad I was eating.

"Just kidding. I'm in Dunwoody," he said, laughing.

I tossed my cloth napkin across the table. His silliness was refreshing. No arguing, no cold beds, or awkward encounters in the kitchen.

"Do you have any kids?" It was his turn to do the asking.

I winked. "Why? Are you offering?"

The brother didn't blink when he answered me. "Yes."

"Okay, you're tripping. So tell me, what happened with your marriage?"

His upbeat demeanor disappeared right before my eyes.

"I loved her too much."

"What exactly does that mean?"

"She just didn't understand me, that's all. I allowed someone to convince her that they were right for her, and just like that, she was gone."

"Well, help me understand you."

A smile crept across his face. "Are we in a session?"

I laughed. "I'm sorry, force of habit. Let's change the subject."

Again came his smile. "No problem."

"So you operate on hearts." I shifted in my chair. "You must have very good hands."

He smiled at my slanted comment; took it the way he wanted to, and nodded.

I shook my head. "I don't see how you can stand there that long, looking at someone's insides."

"You develop a certain kind of numbness toward it. After a while, it becomes about saving or helping them more than it does about the blood and gore," he said.

I looked down at my watch.

Sean asked, "You okay?"

"I'm fine."

"Would you like to go somewhere else?" he asked.

Something about the way he said it made me stop and exhale. The proposition was there with a question mark hanging from it. "I can't. I really need to get home."

"I enjoyed you tonight."

"I enjoyed you too."

"When can I see you again?" he asked.

"I don't know."

"What about tomorrow?"

I thought about it for a second; wanted to say no, but I couldn't. Instead, as he walked me to my car, I told him I would think about it.

"Take down my address, and if you change your mind, I'll be home. I have rounds in the morning, but I am off after that."

I shoved his address in my purse. I gave him my cell phone number and promised to call him as I sped off toward home.

Chapter Eight

The house was quiet when I got home, except for the sound of the television in the guest bedroom.

I made my way up the spiral staircase. The television was watching Donovan as he slept stretched across the guest bed. I thought about waking him up and trying to get him to come to bed with me, but changed my mind.

After taking a shower, I popped two Aleve and pulled on a pair of sweat pants and one of Donovan's oversized T-shirts. Sitting in the middle of the bed Indian-style, I checked the messages that were waiting on our voicemail. There were three hang-ups, and one message from Renee apologizing and asking me to call her. I checked the clock. It was too late to call anyone's house. My thoughts went to my purse, and the small pocket where I had stashed Sean's address.

I kept telling myself that our meeting was innocent. It was nothing like what Donovan had done. Just words. No actions. No betrayal. No disrespect, but I still put his number in my cell phone under the name Susan.

Just in case.

I walked over to the dresser and scanned the pictures of my family and friends. Endless bottles of perfume were neatly resting on top of a gold tray.

My jewelry box was open, showing off the things

Donovan had purchased for me over the years. I dug through it and found a ring that looked like it came from a bubble gum machine. It was fake gold with a fake ruby situated in the middle. I smiled at the memory of him winning it for me at a fair that was in town.

We were dating at the time. He won the ring by knocking down empty milk bottles with a baseball. I was so happy then; thinking we were going to conquer the world. I promised him I would keep the ring forever. He told me to hold on to it until he replaced it with something better. That next summer, he gave me my engagement ring, and the colorful piece of jewelry came to rest in my box.

He told me that he thought I deserved the world, and he was going to give it to me.

A voice came from behind me, causing me to jump and drop the ring. I stared at Donovan's reflection in the mirror.

"You still have that?"

I smiled and bent to pick it up. "Yes. I told you I was going to keep it forever."

"You also told me you would love me forever," he said. "Do you still love me?"

"Yes, I do."

He walked over and stood in my space. Close enough to touch, but not touching just the same. I wanted to reach out and grab him, but I didn't. Time stood still for me. I allowed all of my senses to take him in. From the beauty of his eyes, to the fullness of his lips, to the way his hair curled around his hairline, giving him a sweet, boyish quality. I missed him and he missed me, but neither of us reached out. Instead we just let the moment die.

He turned and headed back toward the hallway. He stopped in the doorway, like a man who wanted to lay down a load of regret and trouble, but kept moving.

***

62

I had only been asleep an hour when my cell phone broke into my dream about Blair Underwood. I cursed whoever it was before answering.

"Hello."

"Did I wake you?"

"Who is this?"

I searched for the clock, and had to squint to focus on the bright red numbers. It was almost two A.M.

"You forgot about me already?"

The voice was familiar. "Sean?"

"I was up, and wanted to see if you were too."

I looked to the hall. No flickering lights, no footsteps. Donovan was asleep. Comfortable with the distance between us, I allowed myself to participate in the late night conversation.

"What are you doing calling me?" I asked. "My husband is here."

"Then why did you answer the phone?"

I didn't have an answer for that.

Our conversation changed from autobiographical to persuasive to borderline perverted. Sean was promising me bubble baths and orgasms, and I was wondering how far I was willing to let him go.

I found myself wondering about another man's touch. He had stirred up something inside of me that I hadn't felt in a long time. The feeling of being wanted—desired.

"I thought you had rounds this morning."

"I do."

"So why are you up, waking me up?"

"I just wanted to let you know that I enjoyed our date."

I yawned. "Is that what that was?"

"Yes, and I want another one."

"Stop playing."

"I'm serious. I can't get you off my mind."

That made me smile.

"I told you, let me think about it, with a *rested* mind."

"After I finish rounds in the morning, and most days, I am usually home around noon. I do that for three days straight, then I am off for forty-eight hours."

"I said I will think about it, Sean."

"Okay." He laughed. "Good night."

"Good night."

I slid out of my bed and made my way down the hall. The door was cracked to the guest bedroom, and I pushed it open just in time to hear Donovan's phone jingle, letting him know he'd just received a text message. The late night interruption caused him to stir, and me to step back into the shadows. I watched him as he read the tiny message on the touch screen before responding, and placing his phone back on the bed next to him.

My jaw tightened. My heart skipped a beat. I didn't want it to.

It just did.

Chapter Nine

It was almost one-thirty and I was sitting in front of a huge art deco house.

I eyed the windows and doors, the intricate detail that was put into the architecture, and the perfectly manicured lawn. All the yards on the street were perfect, despite the ever-falling leaves. I noticed a small sign stuck in the front yard of most of them: DOS ROSAS LANDSCAPING.

Trepidation was telling me to put my car in reverse and drive like the wind; yet needing to see what was behind "door number one" made me turn my ignition off.

I told Eva I was going to be in meetings off-site, and to direct all my calls to my office cell. My schedule was free for the rest of the afternoon, so I decided to take Sean up on his offer.

I put my purse over my shoulder, and cursed myself for not bringing my pepper spray. I pressed the small, dimly lit button, ringing the doorbell. I heard the soft clicks of locks yielding, and swallowed hard.

Sean opened the door.

He was wearing navy blue pajama bottoms and a white wife beater that hugged his hard upper body like it was cut just for him. He stood there and smiled. His body was beautiful. His arms and chest were perfect. A gold chain was resting on his neck, a tiny cross attached to the end.

He had on a pair of small, round-framed glasses that made him look very intelligent, like he was born to live in this high-priced neighborhood with the sign near the gate that said: NEW HOMES! PRICED FROM $750,000.

"Hi."

He smiled. "Hello, Miss Lady."

"Are you busy?"

He licked his lips. "No."

I took a deep breath before looking over my shoulder, then back at him. "Would you like some company?"

For a moment, neither of us said anything. We both knew why I was there, and nobody wanted to make this moment any more uncomfortable. He stepped aside and let me into his world. He locked the door behind us, and led me down a small hallway leading to some steps.

I began to feel heavy as he led me down a staircase to what appeared to be his den. I sunk into the ivory-colored sofa, and placed my purse on the stone coffee table. There were magazines spread across the top: *GQ*, *Ebony*, *JAMA*, and the *Wall Street Journal*.

He stepped behind the bar and stared at me, forcing me to look at him. He asked, "Are you okay?"

"I'm good."

"Would you like something to drink?"

"No, thanks. I'm okay."

I looked around the massive room decorated in things only a surgeon's salary could afford. There was a huge black and white abstract painting over the fireplace. A vase full of fresh red and white roses rested on the mantle.

Lots of African art lined the walls, and beautiful sculptures were in a glass case. I asked him about one sculpture in particular. He told me it was Shona Art,

66

from the Shona tribe in Zimbabwe. It was called *Stone Sculpture of Dancing Lovers*.

"The sculpture, it's beautiful," I said.

"Thank you."

In all the extravagance, the one thing that stood out loud and clear was there was no female presence. I wasn't sure if this was the home they shared or if he moved, but it was obvious he lived alone. He had two glasses sitting on the bar in front of him. He picked them up and walked toward me, never taking his eyes from me.

"What?" I asked.

He handed me a glass, and I tried to pretend I wasn't nervous. I was in another lion's den, and I was as vulnerable as a doe with a broken leg.

"I want you to relax, Miss Lady."

I took the glass from him and eyed the amber-colored liquid in the wineglass. "I told you I didn't want a drink."

His smile was subtle as he winked. "It's apple juice."

I took a sip and laughed. "Thank you."

He sat next to me on the couch, taking my hand in his. I felt his fingers brush my wedding rings, sending a volt of reality through my veins as I slid my hand away and stood up.

This had become all too real, and I was no longer in control. I didn't like that.

He stepped into my path and stopped me. He removed his glasses, and his eyes locked on mine, hypnotizing me and cementing me where I stood. I felt him run his hand up my arm, stopping on my neck before his fingers made their way into my hair.

"Sean, this was a mistake. I—I should go."

"Then why did you come?"

I didn't have an answer, and he knew that. Before I could come up with one, he was kissing me. I felt his hand on my face, and my body relaxed as his tongue searched for mine.

I gave it to him. Opened myself up to him.

He walked me backward until I my back pressed against the wall next to his bar, never taking his lips from mine.

Something inside of me stirred and roared to life. I couldn't seem to catch my breath as his kisses made a trail from my face to my shoulders, and then to my ear.

His voice was serious, intense. "I can't make love to you with your husband in the room."

My head tilted as I tried to figure out what he meant.

"Your wedding rings. Take them off."

I felt like I was having an out of body experience as I slid my rings off and placed them on the edge of his bar. His mouth found the nape of my neck, and a sound escaped my lips, the sound of a woman who needed what this man was offering. Our eyes locked as his hand made its way under my top. The coolness of his flesh immediately called my nipples to attention through the thin fabric of my bra. Emotions that I didn't understand began to swirl around my head.

"You want me to stop?" he asked, all the while running his thumb over my swollen nipple.

I managed to whisper, "No."

Before I could take a deep breath, my jeans were in a pile on the floor, along with my shirt and bra, which were soon joined by his sweats and tee. He reached for me and pulled me to him, seeking out my mouth, and I returned the kiss with all the passion I had. As his hand slipped beyond the waistband of my thong and found the fleshy folds of sensitivity between my legs, I realized that I was at a point of no return. We made our way to the sofa, and he slowly eased me down onto my back, his eyes never leaving mine.

He spoke, "You're beautiful, you know that? Your husband is a lucky man."

Just him mentioning Donovan slowed my roll, but not by much. I loved the feel of his hands as they explored my body. A forbidden, unfamiliar touch that had all of my nerve endings on fire.

Again, his mouth found mine, and in the midst I could hear him tear the wrapper off a condom. That eased my mind even more, and I began to breathe deep in anticipation of what was to come. Almost involuntarily, my legs opened, summoning him, begging him to take me somewhere else.

He positioned himself over me, and slowly I felt him break skin, causing my breath to catch in my throat. He let out a throaty groan as he pushed more of himself into me. He buried his face in the crook of my neck, and gently began kissing and sucking there as his movements became quicker. Quicker, but controlled. He took his time, stirring me and causing my temperature to rise to points I never realized I had.

Before I knew it I told him, "You feel so good."

"You like it?"

"Yes," I sighed.

He picked up the pace, but not by much. Having him inside of me was driving me over the edge somehow; the more he gave, the more I wanted. I was wet. Very wet. I felt my juices running over, taking refuge in the fabric of his couch.

I tried to fight it, but I couldn't, and soon I found myself moaning approval with every thrust. I reached around and grabbed his ass, signifying my agreement of what was happening to my body, the way he was making me feel. I wanted it all. All of it. I spread my legs wider; I wanted him to invade every space that Donovan had avoided by sleeping in the guest room. I wanted him to leave his print all over my insides.

He began to move in and out of me with a steady tempo, with a rhythm that was mind blowing. I felt my orgasm building, and he knew it.

He pressed his lips to my ear; ran his tongue along the sensitive flesh. "I want you to come for me, Teri. Will you do that for me?"

No words were necessary as I came loud and hard. A smile of satisfaction spread across his face as his thrusts became more intense, hitting my sensitive clitoris and prolonging my pleasure. I felt his body tense, and his groan let me know that he too just came.

With our release came the realization—there is no turning back.

When I finally made it home, Donovan was watching television in the den. I made my way toward the kitchen, and tried to find assurance in a bottle of water. I felt a small pang of guilt for what I did. In my mind, this should've made us even, but instead, I had a feeling I'd made things worse.

"Where have you been, Teri?"

"Meetings at the hospital." I kept my back to him; I didn't want him to read my face. I was afraid he would see the kisses of another man.

"I don't believe you."

That did make me turn around. "Excuse you?"

"I tried your office."

My breath caught in my throat. "And?"

"Eva told me that you had a meeting, but you would be back, and I have been calling your cell phone all afternoon."

I closed my eyes and let out a low groan. I didn't tell that twit to tell him I would be back. Where did she get the idea to ad-lib?

"My battery died."

"How convenient."

He got up and walked into the kitchen. I heard the water come on in the sink, then him filling up a glass. He came back into the den.

I took a seat on the couch, still feeling another man's touch on my skin, feeling his lips on mine, and heard the way he begged me to spend the night with him. I thought about the seconds I considered it.

I rubbed my neck. "Can we please talk about this tomorrow?" I pushed past him and made my way up to my bedroom.

In the shower, I rubbed soap over the areas that were kissed by a man other than my husband. My fingers lingered at the spot on my neck that Sean had nibbled on; I ran my hand along my thighs, where he had held me while his tongue danced between my legs.

He had given me orgasms that originated in the soles of my feet, and rode my body like a ride at Six Flags.

I washed my hair, hoping that any traces of Sean would go down the drain with the suds. I ran my fingers down between my legs. The condom we used made me raw. I hadn't used a condom since before I was married. Donovan was the only man I had been with in the last seven years.

My emotions rode a street of guilt, quickly replacing the sexual high that I was previously riding.

I stepped out of the shower and saw my cell phone lighting up on the bathroom counter. The tiny screen told me I had one text.

I couldn't help but smile and think about Sean.

I opened the text, and almost dropped the cell phone in the toilet.

Dr. McCall . . . I didn't know you had it in you. . .

Chapter Ten

I checked my schedule, and my first appointment for the day was with Monica.

I checked her file, refreshing my memory about her case.

I settled in behind my desk and tried to concentrate, but I couldn't. Images from the other afternoon flashed through my mind like a highlight reel on ESPN. I chewed on the end of my pen, smiled at some memories, and cringed at others. I tried calling the number back that had sent me that strange text, but the cell phone was a disposable, and was no longer active. I thought about calling Sean a hundred times, but I was almost embarrassed to hear his voice. Once you have sex with someone, everything changes. The way you see them, the way they see you, your conversations, and your intentions. Everything.

So I settled for calling Renee.

"What happened with your date the other day?"

I told her all about it. All the while, I ignored her smart comments and stupid questions. I told her about the beautiful color of his skin. I also told her about the light brown eyes that were situated under long, dark eyelashes.

"You're crazy," she chastised.

"Whatever."

"Don't whatever me. Did you use a condom?"

I couldn't help but laugh. "What!"

"Come on, Teri," she said. "Who are you trying to convince?"

I sucked my teeth. "Now, you're tripping."

"Look, I know you, and all I'm saying is be careful."

"I know what I am doing. We're just friends."

"Teri, you don't want to make this situation worse. That's all I am saying."

My friend's tone turned disapproving as she tried to reprimand me. She let me know that I should be turning to my husband, not some stranger I met at a fundraiser. I wanted to tell her about the sex, tell her how good he made me feel, but I couldn't.

She wouldn't understand how good it felt to be made love to, not just used for sex. Sean went over every inch of me, not missing a spot. I couldn't have told him to stop if I wanted to. My body had taken over, and told my mind to shut up and sit down. He sexed me up against the wall, before shattering what had to be an orgasm record in the middle of his den.

"Give me a break, Renee. He is just a friend. That's it."

"Yeah, okay." She sighed. "Meet me at the gym tomorrow morning. You sound like you need to relieve some stress."

"What time?"

"Nine, LA Fitness at Atlantic Station," she said.

I agreed, only because it had been a long time since we had gotten together at the gym. We used to meet each other a few times a week, and she would counsel me on my marriage, but that was before she started school part-time. Now she barely had time to be a mother and a wife, let alone a full-time caretaker of my problems and me.

Eva buzzed me to let me know my patient was in the waiting room.

"A'ight, girl. Let me go. My ten o'clock is here."

"Fine! Just abandon me."

"You're a big girl. You'll be fine."

"Whatever, bye!"

"Bye!"

It was almost nine before Donovan came home. I tried to pretend I wasn't waiting for him, but my frustration was obvious when he came in the den. My session with Monica bothered me. When I saw how devastated she was because of her lover, I couldn't help but wonder how Tracie felt when Donovan left, her or if she was even still pursuing him. After all, someone was calling him after hours.

"Where have you been?"

"The office," he said, tossing his keys on the entertainment center.

I had tried him there, and each time his secretary gave me some bogus explanations about him being in meetings, and then leaving for a meeting, then being on conference calls.

"That's bullshit, Donovan. I have been trying to reach you all day!"

He gave me a look like I was agitating him, and said, "I am going to take a shower and lay down."

He turned and headed back toward the foyer and then the staircase. Before I could stop myself, I picked up the bottle of Dasani I had been drinking and threw it in his direction.

It missed him and hit the wall, spilling water all over the white wall and hardwood floor. He spun around, fists balled, ready to fight or defend. I straightened up, braced myself, and got ready to do the same.

"Have you lost your damn mind?" he yelled.

"No, I haven't. You can't just keep dismissing me!"

"What is your problem, Teri?"

"I have a lot on my mind, and I can't even call my husband when I need him."

"Oh, *ahora usted desea jugar a ama de casa! Donde estaba todo ese excedente de la urgencia el último año y una mitad?*" He shouted back. "Not to mention where the hell you were yesterday, Teri? You still haven't answered that question."

"Damn it, Donovan! Speak English!"

I hated when he did that, and he knew it. Seven years of marriage, and I still didn't know a lick of Spanish. I always promised I would make an effort to get to know that side of him, but I never did. Maybe I hadn't given my marriage the hundred percent I bragged about.

"I told you I was at the hospital!" I started to pace the floor. The past year and a half had nothing to do with tonight. Or maybe it had everything to do with it. "I don't know what you want from me."

"I told you."

"Well, damn it, Donovan! Tonight I was here, and you weren't!"

"This is ridiculous!"

"Well, then tell me where you were!"

"I don't have to prove *shit* to you!" my husband said, dismissing the sanctity of our marriage. "And until you answer my question, I am done with this conversation."

Our yelling stopped. We were locked in a glare that could melt the biggest iceberg. Challenging each other, waiting to see who would back down first.

"I'm not doing this anymore. I can't. I don't have the energy." The words barely made it out of my mouth before evaporating into the tension-filled room. Donovan's posture softened. He took a step in my direction then stopped, like something was holding him where he stood. "Teri, if you aren't willing to leave the past in the past and get on with our marriage, then we're simply wasting our time."

He was right, and I knew it. I shook my head, rubbed my temples, and headed upstairs. From my room, I could hear his footsteps in the hall. They stopped in front of our bedroom door before disappearing back down to his end of the hall, to the room where he found peace.

The room without me.

Chapter Eleven

The gym was packed for a Saturday morning.

Everybody and their grandmothers were getting their workout on. As a matter of fact, I saw a few grannies on the treadmills when we came in the door.

I found an empty treadmill, while Renee headed for the bikes. We agreed to meet up in the nine-thirty cardio-kickboxing class.

My warm-up turned into a session. My legs ached as sweat poured from my body. I tried to pound out my frustration with every step I conquered. Every mile was a problem. Work. Donovan. His affair. My miscarriage. I imagined myself happy, with a man who loved and respected me. That man's face changed many times as sweat dripped from my chin and ran down my chest to my wet T-shirt. It changed from Donovan to Sean—hell, then to sexy-ass George Clooney. I didn't discriminate. Whatever the face of happiness was, I wanted it.

I loved my husband, but right now, I didn't like him, and he wasn't very fond of me. I didn't think there was any coming back from that. He didn't want to let go of his hurt, and I wasn't through expressing mine. But I didn't think I was ready to end my marriage either.

After warming up, Renee and I were in the back of a cardio-kickboxing class giggling so hard, my side was aching. We ended up collapsing on a pile of rolled up yoga mats, laughing uncontrollably.

It started when I caught a glimpse of my friend doing her kick move with so much intensity, it came across as comical; then my laughter spread to her.

It felt good to laugh like that. Not thinking about problems—no drama.

She rolled off the mats and stood up. "I am going to swim a few laps."

"I am going to hit the treadmill, then the sauna."

"I will meet you in the showers in about forty-five minutes," she said, wiping her forehead with her towel.

"Okay."

I sweated out the next twenty minutes in a zone on a treadmill. I wanted to force all my tension and anger out through my pores. Sweat ran into my eyes, causing them to sting. I wiped my face with my shirt, and continued to kill my thighs in time with the cardio version of one of Rihanna's tunes blaring from the speakers hanging in the corners of the room.

The wall-length mirror made it seem like there were twice as many people in the room than there really were. The funky fuchsia and green design painted on the wall reminded me of a daycare center. Through my sweat-clouded vision, I looked toward the basketball court through the glass doors. For a moment I thought I spotted Sean, but just as fast as I'd seen him he was gone. I knew when I started hallucinating it was time to end the workout.

After my cool down, I went to the locker room and stripped down to my towel before stepping into the sauna. I was the only one in there, so I took my towel off, spread it across the wooden bench, and tried to sweat off an extra five pounds. I pulled the ponytail holder from my hair and twisted my hair into a bun, getting it off my neck.

I leaned back on the warm wood and let my troubles float above me in the steam. I left them there while I drifted into a nap.

The door to the sauna opened then closed,

causing me to open my eyes. I tried to focus through the steam while wrapping my towel around my naked body. My butt had fallen asleep, so when I stood up, my legs were barely holding me up.

It was hotter than I considered comfortable, and I decided to leave.

I tried the door, but it wouldn't budge. The room was filling with steam and heat. The thermostat was on the outside of the small room, so I couldn't turn it down. I stood on my tiptoes and looked out of the small square window.

The locker room was empty.

I felt my throat getting tight. My eyes were starting to sting as I tried to scan the steam-filled room for something, anything, that would be my saving grace.

"Damn! They need phones in here," I said out loud to no one but my guardian angel, who was obviously slacking on the job.

My skin started to tingle and burn from the heat, and it was getting harder and harder to breathe. I was starting to panic and tried banging on the door. My intense workout coupled with the heat had zapped all my strength, so my banging was more like a toddler's tapping.

I looked out the window again and saw a small white woman wiping down and getting ready to take a shower. I took a deep breath and pulled strength from somewhere and started banging on the door again. I knew if she got in the shower that was it.

She looked up when she heard my knocking and rushed toward the door. When she pulled the door open, the only thing I could do was fall into her tiny frame and hope we both didn't hit the floor.

When I opened my eyes, I was laying on a small cot in the nurse's office at the gym. It reminded me of the small office that our nurse had in high school. That old office was always freezing and smelled like cigarette smoke. Nurse Crooks thought juice and aspirin could cure anything—cramps, headaches, broken bones. That was her remedy.

I was freezing. There were ice packs all around me and a cold cloth on my forehead. I blinked against the brightness of the room. There was a big black guy with a mustache and Nike hat standing near the bed. When he saw me looking at him, he called out to somebody I couldn't see and told them I was awake.

A short, pudgy white lady dressed in a nurse's uniform appeared around the corner. Her hair was pulled in a tight bun and her white stockings made a shushing sound when she walked.

She took the cold cloth from my forehead. For some reason, I locked in on how clear and blue her eyes were. They were unreal.

"How are ya, honey?" she asked, her deep, backwoods Southern accent dripping from every word.

"I'm okay." My voice sounded like a chain smoker's hoarse and scratchy. I tried to sit up, and she put her hand behind my back and helped.

Nurse No Name got me a glass of water. The cool water felt good going down. I tried not to gulp, but I couldn't help it. I gave her the empty glass to refill, this time drinking a little more civilized.

"How'd you go and lock yerself in the sauna?" she asked.

"I—I don't know. I didn't. The door was unlocked when I went in."

"Your friend was mighty worried about you. She's outside. We called the emergency contact on your membership profile."

Renee stuck her head in the small room. "Are you okay? That guy told me you were awake."

"She's fine." The nurse smiled. "Just a little shook up."

Renee asked, "How did this happen?"

"She doesn't know," the nurse said, continuing to

speak for me. "The temperature in that pressure cooker was up high 'nough to cook a roast." She chuckled.

"I'm going to go and get your stuff," Renee said.

I ran my fingers through my damp hair. I felt like I had two layers of sweat coating my skin. I licked my lips; they were salty from the dried sweat.

A few moments later, Donovan walked in and my heart sank to the soles of my feet. He was the last person I wanted to see.

"Hi. How are you?" he asked, addressing the nurse.

"You must be hubby."

He smiled. "Yes, I am."

She retold the colorful story she had just told Renee about me almost cooking myself. Donovan kept his eyes on me the whole time, making me even more uncomfortable.

This was my first time seeing him after our blow up last night. I didn't even know he had left this morning until I got up to get ready for the gym. He left a note telling me he was going to the office and would be home around noon.

The look on his face wasn't one of love or concern. He was mad.

I knew my husband. He was still pissed from last night, and now he was being made to play the doting husband for the public and it was killing him.

"Can I have a moment with my wife?" he asked.

"Sure!" The nurse chuckled. "Just keep the water going in her. If she wants to stay and rest, she can."

The nurse left and Donovan stood back and shoved his hands in the pockets of his Hugo Boss pants. I couldn't lie; he looked good enough for the cover of *GQ*. His cologne filled the room, making my head spin.

He blew out some air and walked to the small window, opened the blinds and looked out.

"What, Donovan?" I swung my legs over the side of the small table.

"Are you okay?"

"Yes. Just a little shaky."

"What happened?"

I told him my version of the story. Explained that I was alone and didn't remember locking the door, from the inside or otherwise.

"Did they see anyone else?"

"No."

"Where was Renee?"

"She told me she was going to the pool."

His eyes scanned the room. He looked like he had something to say, but wasn't sure how to get it out. I slid down off the table and filled my cup with more ice water.

"You can go, Donovan. I know you're busy."

"That's not an issue."

"Look, you obviously don't want to be here. I can get a ride with Renee."

"Is that what you think? Teri, I was scared to death when she called me."

"I don't know what to think. But I do know I am not in the mood for attitude, from you or anyone else. I could have died in that damn box."

"Don't you think I realize that?" he said. "Why do you think I'm so pissed?"

"I just don't want to argue anymore."

There was a tap on the door and Renee stuck her head in. Donovan let out a sound of disgust and shook his head when he saw her.

"I love you too, Donovan," my friend said to him. "Are you okay, Teri?"

I nodded. "Yeah, I'm fine."

"Do you need a ride home?"

"No, Renee, I think I can take my wife home," he said.

It was her turn to shake her head. "Whatever." She turned her attention to me. "Teri, I'll take your bag home and wash your stuff out for you."

I gave a weak smile. "Thanks. I'll call you later."

We rode home in silence. The car seemed to be moving in slow motion. Red lights lasted too long and green lights were hard to come by. Donovan pulled into Quiktrip for gas. I took that opportunity to check my phone.

I had two missed calls.

Both from Sean.

Chapter Twelve

I waited for Donovan to fall asleep before I tried calling Sean.

I hadn't talked to him since I left his house a few days ago, sexually satisfied and emotionally heavy. He left me one message apologizing for being so hard to pin down. He blamed his hectic schedule at the hospital, but secretly, I thanked it.

"You are so beautiful," he said.

"Why do you keep telling me that?"

"Because it's true."

Our conversation seemed to be the Tylenol I needed. I relaxed into my kingless king-size bed and let his voice wash over me.

"Can I take you to lunch tomorrow?"

"You're joking, right?"

"No, I like your company, Teri. Call me when you get up. I should be done with surgery around eleven."

"Okay."

The next afternoon, we met at the Alantic Grill at Atlantic Station.

Sean had on black slacks and a crew neck long-sleeve shirt with his sleeves pushed up, showing his forearms. I kept it simple with a blue jean knee-length skirt, a long sleeve V-neck tee, topped off with my waist-length black leather jacket and calf-high boots. My hair was loose and hanging down my back. For the first time in a long time, I felt attractive and my mood reflected that.

The waitress at Atlantic Grill led us to a table near the window. We ordered drinks and watched people pass by. We chatted for the better part of an hour about nothing and everything. I told him how I was thinking about quitting my job to pursue dancing.

"Oh, you're a dancer?"

"I used to be," I said, as a slight smile spread across my face. "But, times change . . . people change."

"No, Miss Lady, time stays the same, waiting for no one; it's the people who change."

His words were like liquid truth, invading me and making me see things differently. I looked into his eyes. Tried to find a hint of crazy, but kept coming up empty. There was something about this man that was making me crave him in the worst way.

"So, what's up with you and your husband?" he finally asked.

I couldn't help but shift around in my seat. I knew this question was coming. Even though he knew I was married, he never brought it up in our phone conversations, which I actually appreciated.

"I don't know."

"Do you think you two will work it out?"

"Sometimes."

"What does that mean?"

I sighed. "Sometimes I do, but there are other times when I am not sure that I want to."

"Example."

"Like now, when I'm sitting here talking to you." I looked around the restaurant. Guilt was in the room, circling, threatening to pounce like a hungry tiger and tear me apart.

"Am I a distraction?"

"You know you are."

"So why do you keep taking my calls?"

I stared into my watered-down sweet tea. "Because I like you."

"I like you too."

I got lost in his smile as he reached across the table and touched my hand.

When we finished, we walked the streets, stopping at all the vendors. I spotted a cute bracelet from an older lady who made everything by hand.

"This is really pretty," I said, holding up the small bracelet decorated with tiny crystals.

"Then you should have it."

I shook my head. "Sean, seriously, you don't have to buy me this."

"I know, but I want you to have it."

He bent down and kissed my lips. Soft. Like a lover would. A chill rode my spine as he sat me on the small stool and placed the trinket on my wrist.

"Thank you," I said as we walked toward the cotton candy vendor.

"No problem. Now you owe me."

"Owe you what?"

"Not now, but I'll let you know."

After we left the downtown, we drove up Linden Avenue and found a parking space on the street. We walked two blocks to Gladys Knight's spot and found a cozy booth tucked in the corner, where we ordered coffee. I got a sinking feeling in the pit of my stomach. I checked my watch and realized that my coach was about to turn into a pumpkin. I didn't want this to end. My cell phone vibrated against the table.

"You can answer it," he said.

I looked at the caller ID. My husband's work number came up. I took a deep breath before answering it.

"Hello?"

"Teri, we need to talk."

"Why? Do you have another set of divorce papers for me?"

86

Sean got up and went to the bathroom, giving me some privacy.

"Contrary to what you are thinking Teri, I am not the enemy here. But you do need to bring your ass home."

I tensed. "Yeah, okay."

"I'll see you when you get home." He hung up and left me sitting with a heart heavy with conflict.

Sean's voice was the only sound I heard. I hadn't even noticed he was back from the bathroom. "Are you okay?"

I just nodded, swallowed the last of my sweet tea, and reached for my purse.

"I have to go."

He grabbed my hand. "Wait, Teri. You don't have to go. Talk to me."

I sank back into my seat, ran my fingers through my hair, and tried to avoid eye contact with him. I wanted Sean to take me away and make all of my problems go away.

"There is nothing to talk about. There are just some things I need to clear up before I leave the office tonight."

"Well, at least let me drive you to your car."

When I got back to the office, it was quiet. It was late and everyone was behind closed doors dealing with someone else's problems.

I made my way past Dr. Lee's office. He had asked me several times if I was ready to make a decision yet, so I had been avoiding him like the plague. Harrison was finishing up with his patient, and waved as he walked him to the front.

I smiled and disappeared into my office.

The rest of my afternoon went smoothly. I clock-watched as I listened to Mr. Wendell tell me about his week.

"Did you do the exercise I gave you last week, Mr. Wendell?"

"Oh, no," he said, vigorously shaking his head. "I don't think I can do that."

"Okay, okay. That's fine. But I think you are ready for this one. I really do. The circus is only going to be in town for three more days."

I heard the soft chime of my clock, letting me know that this torturous hour was finally over. I picked up a white envelope that was resting on my desk and handed it to Mr. Wendell.

"These are the box seats at Philips Arena. You will be far enough away from the floor to make an attempt at facing your fear."

He slowly took the tickets, assuring me he wasn't ready.

I patted his back as he left. "You'll be fine, Mr. Wendell. See you next week. Bring me back a souvenir."

The phone on my desk rang and I ran to get it. I had been waiting all day for this phone call.

"Hey, Miss Lady." Sean's voice was just what I needed to hear. He was right on time. I settled in behind my desk.

"How is that bracelet working out for you?"

"I love it."

"Can I see you before you go home?"

"I can't, Sean," I said.

I got up and walked over to the huge window overlooking downtown. I locked in on a car zooming down Peachtree Street and wondered if the people inside were happy. If life had given them what they'd been promised or if their life was as screwed up as mine.

"Why?" he asked. His voice was low and heavy with lust.

I sighed. "I have to go home and see what's going on with my husband. He says he wants to talk."

I heard the door open and close behind me. I spun around and Sean was standing in my office.

I hung up my cell and laid it on my desk. "What are you doing here?"

I stood frozen as I watched him turn the small lock on the door handle. My heart was beating so fast I thought I was going to pass out. He had changed clothes. Now, he was in jeans and a Sean John sweater. My mouth opened slightly to say something, but nothing came out. I didn't know if I should be scared or flattered that he had tracked me down.

I made a move toward the door and he stepped in my path. My breath caught in my throat as his hand slid up my arm toward my neck.

"Sean, you can't be here. I have to get ready to go," I managed, barely above a whisper.

He wasn't saying anything, which was starting to scare me. The look in his eyes was indescribable. It was like he was looking at me and through me all at the same time. I looked around the office for anything that was in arm's reach to defend myself with if I had to. Just as I spied my stapler, his hand reached up and he had a tight grip on my throat. I reached up and grabbed his wrist.

Tears stung my eyes. "What are you doing?"

"I'm not gonna hurt you." He kissed my lips. "Not unless you want me to."

Without hesitating, my mouth yielded to his kiss. I sucked his tongue as he ran his hand down my side and began to pull my skirt up. He broke our kiss and made his way down to my neck. I could barely breathe, let alone tell him to stop.

He sunk down, picked me up, and placed me on the edge of my desk.

"I can't do this, Sean."

"Just let me taste you; then you can go home to him."

His lips found mine again as he pushed my skirt up around my thighs. I felt my legs parting, giving him access to what he wanted. He lifted me off the desk and slid my panties off. My warm flesh on the cool desk excited me even more. For a brief moment, I wanted to know what he had told Eva to get past her, but when his finger broke through my moist folds, I didn't care if she'd just let Charles Manson in my office.

Our kiss became intense as he continued to finger me, causing my wetness to seep out onto my mahogany desk. His index finger massaged my g-spot as he gently sucked on my neck.

He pressed his lips against my ear. "I want you to be mine, Teri."

Before I could say anything, my body started to tremble as I came all over my desk and his hand.

He kissed me. "Your body wants me, Teri."

I tried to catch my breath as he knelt down and positioned himself between my legs. He grabbed the backs of my thighs and pulled me toward him. He began planting kisses on my inner thighs. The gentle kissing and sucking was driving me crazy. He slid a finger inside and began stirring my juices. Beads of sweat formed on my forehead and my breathing became erratic when he found my spot again and began massaging it back to attention.

"Sean—"

Before I could finish, he reached up and put his moist finger in my mouth. I sucked my juices off while his tongue licked around my edges. He reached down and opened me up to him. He began running circles around my inner lips, driving me crazy. His tongue developed a rhythm that was mind-blowing. My body trembled with each gentle tug of my sensitive lips.

"Ummm." I let out a moan. I tried to be as quiet as I could, but he was making it hard. My eyes shot to the door, making sure it was indeed locked.

He stopped lapping and began gently sucking on my swollen clit.

"Come for me, Teri," he demanded.

I felt my legs start to quiver as my orgasm built.

"Oh . . . my . . . God, Sean." My body was on fire. He pressed down on my bud with the flat of his tongue then gently sucked it into his mouth, sending me over the top. I let out a low scream as I released, again, but this time into his mouth.

He rose to his feet, licking my essence from his lips. While my breathing returned to normal, I tried to readjust my clothes.

I wiped the sweat from my brow with the back of my hand. "I can't believe I just did that."

He walked over and kissed me, giving me a taste of my own juices. I sucked his tongue, became intoxicated off of him. I could feel the bulge in his pants, which made me back up a little.

I smiled. "I really need to go, Sean." I checked my watch; it was almost six. I made my way around my office to get ready to leave.

"You don't have to go home to him, Teri."

"Yes, I do. Regardless, he's still my husband."

"Why don't you just leave?"

"I can't just do that."

"Why not? People do it every day. My wife did it to me."

I wasn't sure how to respond to that, so I just got quiet.

"Do you want to talk?" he asked.

I shoved my cell phone in my purse. "Sean, I owe it to our marriage to hear him out."

He blew out some air, and I could see the anger spreading across his face.

"I'll call you as soon as I can," I said.

"Whatever, Teri." He turned and walked out of my office, leaving me standing in the midst of confusion and lust.

I made my way home, and when I saw the lights on in the den, I wanted to turn and run for the hills. The television could be heard before I even got into the house.

He looked up when I walked in the room. "Hey."

I tossed my purse on the couch. "So, what did you want to talk about?" When I sat down on the couch, I realized that I still didn't have on any panties. My thighs were moist and my sex was throbbing from the workout Sean had given it.

"Us . . . this marriage . . . there's a lot at stake here."

"I know."

His tone was condescending. "So what? You want to give our marriage a chance?"

I sighed and tried to get my thoughts together. "Yes . . . no . . . I don't know."

"You need to figure it out. You can't continue to live here, doing the things you're doing."

I licked my lips, tasted what another man had left behind. "What are you talking about?"

He handed me an envelope, one of the brown ones big enough to hold an 8 x 10.

My confusion grew. I asked, "What is this?"

Anger flashed across his face. "Open it!"

As I ran my finger under the flap, my heart started racing when I realized they were pictures. I blinked a few times and tried to will the images away. I wanted the pictures to burn and wilt in my hands, but they didn't. I didn't want the woman in them to be me, but she was. They were pictures of me having sex with another man.

Sean was harder to make out, but there was no mistaking me and the tattoo on my lower back. My mouth got dry and my hands started to shake. I tried to steady them as I slid the pictures back into the envelope.

Donovan read my expression. Then he spat out, "What the fuck is that, Teresa?"

I found a voice, but it was weak. "Donovan, please, let me explain."

He spoke through clenched teeth. "Explain what? How you slept with another man, and all this time you been riding me? Making me live out the guilt of what I did damn near daily for the last six months?"

"Donovan, wait."

"How long, Teri?"

"Would you let me explain?" I begged, fighting tears.

"How long!"

"Donovan, please let me—"

"You want to explain?" he shot back. "I don't need a sex education lesson, Teri! I know what is going on in those pictures. My wife is getting *fucked* by another man!"

His eyes burned holes through me. At that moment, I wished that I hadn't followed a broken heart to Dunwoody. I took a step toward my husband and he backed away. I tried to hold back the flood of tears and sobs that were threatening to take over my body.

"Teri, look at the pictures!" His booming voice caused me to jump, and I looked down at the disaster hidden in the envelope I was holding in my trembling hands. I pulled them out and I flipped through them, not really looking at them, but unable to blind myself to the images. They showed Sean and me in the den on the floor, and him kissing me good-bye when I left that day.

He continued, "How can you possibly explain that? You *can't* explain that."

"Where?" I tried to speak, but couldn't get it to come out.

He flashed a sinister smile. "You want to know where I got them?"

I nodded.

Just as fast his smile disappeared. "A fucking concerned citizen!" He continued pacing. "A messenger dropped them off this afternoon."

"Messenger?" I was struggling with confusion and anger.

"Yes, Teri. At my office!!" He ran his fingers

through his curly locks. "What if Helen had opened this envelope before me, Teri?"

His anger was strong enough to crack the foundation of our house. I flinched at each inflection of his voice as I moved closer to the door leading to the hallway. Before I could make a break, he grabbed my neck and slammed me against the wall.

"Donovan, I am sorry! Please!"

He pointed toward the doorway. "Get out!"

"Donovan, please, wait!"

That's when I noticed he had already packed my suitcases and had them waiting in the den. He tossed them in my direction as he continued to evict me from our home.

"I want you out of here, Teri. *Now!*"

"Where am I going to go?" I was crying so hard I couldn't see straight. My chest was tight, and my breathing was becoming difficult.

"I don't know! Go to that nigga's house. I really don't care."

"Please, Donovan, don't do this."

"I don't want to hear it. What you did was wrong on every level, Teresa. You were being vindictive! A mistake is a mistake, but wrong is wrong."

I didn't have a defense for anything. He was right. I looked down at the floor; pictures were scattered between the den and the living room. Part of me wanted to pick them up and burn them, but I couldn't move.

"You know, Teri—when I started getting phone calls telling me that you were cheating, I didn't want to believe it."

That got my attention. "What phone calls? When?"

My mind was racing. Who sent him the pictures? Who had been calling him? Was it Sean?

"I let them go—didn't want to make waves because I trusted my wife. I knew there was no way she would do this to our marriage. Not Teresa." He continued to talk, ignoring my question.

"What phone calls, Donovan?" I demanded.

"They started about two weeks ago," he said. "Voicemails mostly, but I didn't feed into it. Guess I should've kept you on a shorter leash, huh?"

"Donovan, please," I continued to beg.

"Get out, Teresa!"

Wave after wave of emotion rode me as I struggled to load the suitcases into my car through tears. My world was spiraling out of control and I couldn't stop it. So many thoughts clouded my mind. Images of how life used to be and foresight of how life was going to be. I stumbled and almost fell carrying the last bag to the trunk as Donovan stood in the door, watching me and yelling at me in both English and Spanish.

"*Perra de* trifling! I don't *desea verle siempre otra vez!*"

Neighbors had come out and others were peeking out of their windows to get a look at the commotion. I made eye contact with the doctor who lived next door. He just turned and walked back inside of his perfect world.

An hour later, I was standing on Renee's doorstep crying, hoping my friend would take me in without asking a lot of questions. I thought about going to Sean's, but that would have only made the situation worse. I needed to get my head together. I knew Donovan would be quick with the divorce papers, so I was going to have to find an attorney of my own.

Renee fixed me a cup of tea, and I filled her in on the important parts and listened to her scold me about things that I didn't think were important.

"I told you not to mess with that man." She scratched her head. "Damn, *pictures*, Teri? I hope you used protection."

"Renee, please, not right now. Can I stay here or not?"

She sank into the chair across the kitchen table from me. "Of course you can. But you need to figure out what you are going to do."

"I don't know. I'm sure Donovan is going to do everything he can to get those papers in my hands now, and probably take me for everything."

"He won't do that."

I leaned back in my chair. "And to top it off, Sean is mad at me."

"What is his problem?"

"He wanted me to come over and I didn't. Instead I went home and ended up being evicted. Maybe I should've picked door number two."

"You did the right thing, regardless of the outcome. His dumb ass has no claim on you. Let him be mad. Donovan needs to be your focus right now."

I shook my head, trying to fight a splitting headache and a whole lot of guilt. I was on the verge of an emotional breakdown and I couldn't afford that right now.

My cell phone vibrated against the wooden table. I watched it dance until it stopped.

It beeped, letting me know there was a message.

"Why didn't you answer that?"

"I am not in the mood for either one of them right now." I took a sip of the tea, closed my eyes, and tried to rub away the knot that was growing in my shoulder.

"Who do you think took the pictures?"

I shrugged and shook my head.

"Do you know who would've called him?"

I shook my head. "I mean, who would want to do something like that?"

"What about Sean? You think he would do this to break up you and Donovan?"

"I doubt it."

"Well, somebody's got it in for you."

"Yeah, obviously." I ran my fingers through my tangled hair.

"You sure you're gonna be okay?"

I nodded.

"There is just a lot of tension in that house right

now. I need to be as far away from there as possible. I just want to lie down and go to sleep."

"You can have the room next to Christopher."

"Thank you."

After I got settled into her guest room, I decided to take a hot shower. The bathroom filled with steam as I undressed.

I looked at myself in the mirror and hated what I saw. I was turning into someone I didn't like, and I felt like I had no control over the transformation that was taking place.

Once in the shower, I let the water run through my hair and down my body. I blinked against tears that kept coming, burning my eyes. I washed my hair slowly, inhaled the strong smell of perfumed soap and tried to calm my nerves. I stepped out and dried off before pulling on one of Derrick's T-shirts.

I wanted to wake up and have all of this be a dream.

The cold confines of a strange bed let me know that it wasn't.

I reached for my cell and dialed Sean.

Chapter Thirteen

It had been almost two weeks since I'd heard from Donovan.

I honestly wasn't ready to hear what he had to say anyway, no matter what it was, so I wasn't heartbroken. I had even managed to stay out of the way of Renee and all her words of wisdom. I found the name of a good attorney that I put on retainer, just in case.

Sean was a good shoulder and ear. I felt bad for unloading my issues on him, but he had this way of making me feel as though no matter what, everything would be okay. I opened up to him about my passion for dancing, I even sent him some pictures from a few of my recitals when I was younger. It was nice to talk to someone in the medical profession that understood the demands rather than fought against them.

I rescheduled all my appointments, essentially taking the day off, and headed to the mall. I needed to breathe. I didn't want to be cooped up in my office all afternoon. I decided to send Dr. Lee an informal e-mail officially accepting his offer, and told him we could go over details next week.

I walked the near-empty Lenox Square Mall and ended up spending way too much on a pair of Jimmy Choos and a silk scarf to match a suit I had bought a few weeks before.

The food court was full of the usual lunchtime crowd. I grabbed a slice of cheese pizza and a diet Pepsi and found a table that was tucked in the corner so I could people watch. I looked at all the lunch cliques that were gathering in front of the various places to eat. Everyone seemed to gravitate toward the Chinese buffet.

My wedding rings sparkled on my left hand and reminded me that I had problems that not even a pair of shoes and a scarf could make better.

I never meant for Donovan to find out. And definitely not the way he had.

I chose the wrong path in looking for my happiness, and now I was about to pay the ultimate price and lose everything I had worked so hard for. After my miscarriage, I threw myself into my work and forced myself to forget. As a psychologist I knew better, but Donovan withdrew into his work as well. There were many nights I ached for him, needed him to be a husband, and he wasn't there. I hardened myself to what was going on in my home, and found my own way to cope with it.

I was watching a bunch of teenagers cackle over a spread of Taco Bell and Chinese food when my cell rang. I didn't recognize the number, but decided to answer it anyway.

"Dr. McCall."

"Good afternoon, Doctor."

I smiled a little. "Hello, Sean."

"Where are you?"

"Out at the mall getting some retail therapy."

"Everything okay?" he asked.

"It could be better."

"Come down to the hospital and see me."

"Sean, you're part of my problem right now."

"What do you mean?" he asked, getting defensive.

"It's complicated." I wanted to tell him about the pictures, but decided against it. This was my fight, and as long as Donovan didn't know him or who he was, I was good.

"Just come see me, so we can talk."

Against my better judgment I agreed. Twenty minutes later I was pulling my car into the parking deck at Crawford Long and found a space near the small elevator. I waited for Sean to emerge from the red doors marked with the number one.

I checked my reflection in the mirror and made sure that I looked presentable. Other than the puffiness around my eyes from crying, I looked halfway decent. I caught a glimpse of him in my rearview. He was still wearing his blue scrubs and a white lab coat; his stethoscope was draped around his neck. Something about seeing him like that made me smile.

He leaned in my driver's side window. "Hello, Miss Lady."

"Wow. You look real cute in your scrubs."

He chuckled and looked down at his clothes. He nodded. "Yep, that's why I spent over a hundred grand to graduate from medical school, so I could look cute in this outfit."

"Are you ready to go?" I asked.

He looked back toward the door he just came from. "Actually, I am waiting on labs for one of my patients; then I'll be ready. Why don't you meet me at my house?"

"Excuse me?"

He handed me a set of keys. "Meet me at my house."

I smiled and took the keys. "How are you going to get in?"

"Hopefully, you'll be there to let me in." He winked.

"Touché."

He touched my cheek.

"Are you okay?"

"I'm fine."

"Good."

"I'll make you feel much better later."

I cracked a smile. "I can't wait."

"Neither can I."

100

My phone rang twice on my way up Interstate 285. Renee called to let me know she was leaving a key under the plant on her back deck. The second call was from home. My heart wanted me to answer, but I just wasn't there yet mentally. I wasn't ready to have that talk.

You know, the talk—it's not you it's me, maybe if we had met later in life, I am moving out, yadda yadda yadda.

I unlocked the door to Sean's house and placed the keys on the small table that lined the foyer wall. I put my purse on the coffee table, and opened the curtains. The midday sun was high in the sky, heating up the air. I searched the wall for the thermostat, found the small digital box, and set it to a cool sixty degrees.

I made my way down the hall.

I was a lost soul in a strange house.

The warm chocolates, mochas, and tans of the décor were calming.

I climbed the staircase and made my way down the long hallway. There were rooms on both sides, but the landing opened up to a balcony that overlooked the living room. The layout reminded me of Romeo and Juliet. The first time I had been here, I never made it to this part of the house. We never left the den.

I couldn't help but smile at that memory. I headed down the hall toward the double doors situated at the end.

My hand rested on the doorknob. I looked over my shoulder and made sure no one was coming before I stepped into the massive bedroom. Inside was a huge California king bed situated in the middle of a room that was damn near made of windows. The windows overlooked the backyard with a huge pool.

I ran a finger across the top of the cherry dresser. No dust. I headed over to the doors that led to the balcony. I stepped out onto the landing and took a deep

101

breath. The air surrounding me seemed crisp, clearer. I pulled out my cell and dialed Donovan. He answered on the first ring.

Here I was a married woman, sneaking around another man's house. As nice as the house was, on every level it was pathetic—no matter how beautiful the view was.

"Where are you?"

"I'm gone. That's what you wanted, right?"

"Teri, what did you expect?"

"What I didn't expect was for you to put me out, Donovan. I think we just need some time apart. You know—some time to get our heads together. I'll call you in a few days."

"Where are you?"

"On my way to Renee's."

He let out a sigh.

I spun around when I heard Sean's footsteps.

"I'll call you later, Donovan." I closed my phone and forced a smile on my face.

Sean smiled. "Glad to see you made it."

"I'm sorry," I said. "I was just—"

"Snooping around my house?" He chuckled.

I laughed, looking around his bedroom. "How's your patient?" I asked.

"He's fine. Thanks for asking."

He was still in doctor mode, dressed in his scrubs, but no lab coat. He walked to his closet and took out a white cotton robe.

He smiled at me. "You look good standing there."

I looked at him, confused. "What do you mean?"

"You fit perfectly." He asked, "Do you mind if I take a shower? I smell like hospital."

I shook my head. "I can wait downstairs."

He pulled his shirt over his head. "You don't have to. There's a TV room down the hall." He smiled. "Or have you found that already?"

I chuckled. "No. I haven't."

He leaned in and kissed my lips. "I'll see you in a minute."

I made my way to the TV room. There was nothing special about the room at first glance. I tapped the button on the wall and tried to find the light switch. Soft, dim track lighting illuminated the room, exposing the black furniture and décor.

I looked around, trying to find the TV to go with this TV room, but there wasn't one. I ran my hand along the wall and found a small switch; it was so small it was almost flush with the wall. I tapped it. I turned around just in time to see the 42-inch flat screen built into the wall above the fireplace come to life.

"You have got to be kidding me," I whispered to myself. I couldn't believe that his wife left all of this. Their marriage must have been really screwed up for her to give him and all of this up.

I sank into the soft leather of the oversized chair, then found the remote situated in the armrest. I was about to settle on watching a rerun of HOUSE OF PAYNE when my cell vibrated in my purse. I looked at the display. It was my office. I checked the time and noted it was almost three o'clock.

I answered. "Dr. McCall."

"Hello, Teri. This is Eva."

"Hello, Eva."

"They called a staff meeting around four. Dr. Lee told me to call and let you know."

"I don't think I am going to make it in, Eva," I said. "I am not feeling well."

"What do you want me to tell them?" she asked.

"Tell them I am puking my guts out and I will see them tomorrow."

I hung up—,not giving her a chance to make me feel worse than I already did for lying. I looked at my phone and saw the little envelope in the corner letting me know I had unread text messages.

Teri, this is Donovan. Call me.

I rubbed my forehead and looked around another man's home. I took it all in as I listened to my husband beg for me to come home.

The next message was from Renee.

Teri, what the hell is up with you? Call me.

I wasn't in the mood for her preaching, so I deleted her message immediately.

The last one was another message from my husband. My heart ached for him and for our marriage.

Te amo, Teri. Vengo por favor a casa.

I closed my eyes at the sight of that message. I could hear the voice of my husband asking me to come home, telling me he loved me.

That wasn't hard to translate. That I understood.

I started to dial my home number. It rang once, but Sean walked in the room. I ended the call and shoved my phone back in my purse.

He was no longer Mr. Medicine. He had changed into a pair of jeans and a T-shirt that read: MOREHOUSE SCHOOL OF MEDICINE.

He was relaxed. The way a man should be in his home.

He placed two pagers on the smoked glass coffee table. One pager was black and the other red.

"Why do you have two pagers?" I asked.

"One is the ER, the other is my on call pager," he answered.

"Why two different pagers for the same hospital?"

"If the ER pager goes off, that's an immediate date killer. No call backs. I have to jet to the hospital." He laughed. "If my on call pager goes off, that's just a call back. It's usually a nurse with a question about meds or vitals or something. Let's hope neither happens tonight," he said.

He walked to the small mini bar and got a bottle of water from the fridge. "Are you okay?"

I lied. "Yeah, I'm okay."

"Are you hungry?"

"A little."

"Chinese?"

I managed a smile. "Sounds good."

"What time do you have to be at work?"

"I am not going in today. Too much on my mind."

"So I have you for a little while?"

I just smiled and nodded. The lump in my throat wouldn't allow me to speak. In fact, it threatened to choke me.

"You want to talk about it?"

"Not really . . . kind of weird talking about my husband with you. I think that we should keep him and my marriage off limits."

He held up his hands. "Fair enough." He nodded toward my hand.

I couldn't help but chuckle as I slid the platinum and diamonds off my finger and slid them in my purse.

We munched on egg rolls and sweet and sour chicken while we watched *Ocean's Eleven*. I told him it was one of my favorites, so he dug it out of his collection.

"The way they pulled that off was bananas!" He laughed.

"Tell me about it."

"Do you think you could ever do anything like that?" he asked.

"Who me," I asked. "No, not me. I'm a chicken."

That made him laugh. His relaxed demeanor and his openness helped me push my frustrations aside. For hours, we sat on the floor and talked. He tried to get me to dance for him, but the only person I had ever danced for privately was Donovan.

His tone was intense, caring. "Tell me, Teri, what is it that he isn't doing?"

"What?"

"Your husband has to be doing something off the wall to drive you away."

Against my better judgment, I told him everything. I told him about the miscarriage and Donovan's affair. Basically, I slit my wrists emotionally right there on the man's couch.

"Oh, so he cheated on you?"

I nodded, unsure of how he saw me. I was a woman betrayed, but I was still a married woman who was now betraying. I got up, went to the bar, and poured myself a glass of Zinfandel.

He asked, "Am I some sort of revenge?"

I shook my head. "No."

He stood up and I could tell he was a little agitated.

"Sean, I think I need to go. It's getting late."

"No, you can't leave."

I turned around and shot him a look. "What do you mean I can't leave?"

He stood up and headed toward the door. "Wait here. I'll be right back."

He disappeared and left me alone with my frustrations. I never set out to hurt Donovan, but sometimes a broken heart will make you do stupid things. It clouds your judgment, and makes you think up is down and right is left.

He came back in and looked at his watch. "Let's go for a ride."

"Where?"

"I can't tell you that."

"Why?"

He raised an eyebrow. "Do you want to go or not?"

I agreed. For some reason, I trusted him. I had convinced myself that what was going on wasn't wrong. It wasn't an affair in my eyes.

He was helping me, comforting me, and making the hurt go away.

Chapter Fourteen

We drove on I-20 going west.

The night air mingled with the sexual tension in the air, blowing it around the inside of his Range Rover. Sean reached over and took my hand. He held it like it was his, like I was where I should be—by his side.

We made a left on Fulton Industrial, just on the flip side of the hood that was Bankhead Highway. Fast food restaurants and gas stations, along with substandard businesses, lined the wide highway. He pulled into an Amoco and ran in, re-emerging with a bottle of water for me. I was getting nervous and my throat was getting dry.

He asked, "You okay?"

"I would be great if you told me where we were going."

"Patience." He leaned across the console and kissed me. Electricity ran through my veins as he ran his hand up my thigh.

I said, "I hope wherever it is, it's close."

He chuckled. "Do you trust me?"

I nodded like I had been hypnotized.

He drove a couple blocks before making a left and heading up a long, winding road that was a dead end. The building was big and black with no signs outside.

We walked around the back of the building; he opened the door, and had me walk in.

The corridor was dimly lit, so I grabbed his hand. Actually, I held on for dear life. There was no way he was going to let me go.

We walked into a room that was brightly lit. There was a huge black curtain on one side, and a dancer's bar lined the mirrored wall on the other.

"What is this?"

"I have a friend who owed me a favor."

I smiled. "Why are we here?"

"I want you to dance for me."

"Excuse me?"

"I want to see you dance."

He motioned toward a changing room and told me I could change in there.

"Change into what?"

"Everything is back there for you. Now go ahead," he said, laughing.

I walked slowly toward the changing area, pulled mostly out of instinct and curiosity. I had never danced for anyone but Donovan, and that was something that I always thought was special.

I touched the soft pink garments that were waiting for me. My mind was racing. How in the world did he put this all together? Why would he go through all this trouble just for me? This was crazy. The whole situation was crazy.

The satin toe shoes were a beautiful shade of pink, and he had actually gotten the size right. My adrenaline started flowing as I quickly changed into the skirted Eurotard dance dress and admired myself in the mirror. I dug around in my purse, found a brush, and brushed my hair up into a bun.

I smiled at my reflection. It was of a woman I hadn't seen in a long time.

I stepped out from behind the changing curtain and the dance floor was all mine. I could hear Sean's voice. "Are you ready?"

"I guess so. Where are you?"

The black curtain slowly slid back, opening the room up to a very small auditorium. I spotted Sean sitting dead center of the first row of the empty room.

"I don't think I can do this."

"Yes, you can. You're going to be great."

"I haven't danced in years. I thought I was going to just play around and dance for you."

He winked. "You can do that later."

I laughed. He got up and walked to the other side of the stage and *Swan Lake*'s "Dance of the Swans" started playing. He motioned for me to go ahead and dance as he reclaimed his spot in the front row.

The music took over my body and soul. I started moving and I didn't want to stop. Ever. I pulled emotion and passion from a place deep inside. I allowed myself to block out everything and find myself inside the dance. And I did. I loved what I had found. I loved her.

When I finished, Sean walked toward me in the middle of the stage with roses in hand. It felt so good from the energy of the music to the way the dancing got my heart pumping.

He hugged me and told me how good I was.

"Thank you," I said, wiping sweat from my forehead.

"Are you hungry?"

I smiled. "Famished."

The smoothness of his skin, the almond shape of his eyes, his scent—they were all intoxicating. I wanted him so badly. I needed him, and on some level, I needed to believe he needed me.

He kissed me deeply. Our bodies were so close that I could feel his manhood straining against his pants, begging to get out. The warmth between my legs was crying to be filled.

"Take me home," I managed between kisses.

After I changed, we barely made it to the truck. The ride up I-285 was unforgiving. He reached over and ran his hand up my thigh until he reached what he was looking for. I spread my legs, giving it to him. I laid back, closed my eyes, and let him rub me there until I exploded in his passenger seat.

His Range Rover swerved and we got off on Bolton Road. I looked at Sean. He was concentrating trying to satisfy the same want that I had.

We pulled into an office park and he found a space between two semi trucks.

Words weren't necessary. We were like teenagers after a high school football game. He hit a button and slid my seat all the way back before reclining his. I heard the buckle on his belt as I wiggled out of my jeans. I was taken over by lust, driven by a need.

"I want you," he breathed.

"Take me."

He pulled me on top of him, lifted my hips and guided himself into me, taking all I had to offer. For a split second, I realized that we were flesh to flesh as his warmth eased into me, filling me. He felt so good; I didn't want him to stop, not even to put on a condom.

His jaw tightened as I began to slowly move against him. He told me how good I felt.

"I love what you did for me tonight."

"Is that right."

"Uh-hmm." I moaned. "You feel good."

He smiled. "A perfect fit. I want you, Teri. I want you in my life."

For a second, that slowed my pace. I rotated my hips slowly, staring into his eyes. I slowed my groove. Savored the feeling of him.

"Sean, I—"

Before I could say anything, he took control grabbing my hips and creating a rhythm so mind blowing that I couldn't hold off the orgasm that was riding my back. I came so hard that my head started spinning. He closed his eyes and threw his head back as he bit his lower lip. He let out a loud growl and released. We stayed like that while we caught our breath.

"Oh my goodness."

He smiled. "Tell me about it. You are incredible, you know that?"

He kissed me.

"So are you."

My phone vibrated on the seat, snatching me back to reality. I watched the red light blinking antagonizing me.

"Do you want to answer that?"

I shook my head before resting it on his shoulder. "Not really."

"Then don't."

We made it back to his house and showered. He washed me from head to toe and made me feel beautiful. He told me he wanted me to stay with him as he rubbed lotion on my back.

"You know I can't do that."

"Why not? He doesn't know how to take care of you."

I sat up and pulled the towel over my bare body. "And you do?"

"You know what I mean."

"No, why don't you tell me?"

He sighed. "I just meant that he can't love you like I can."

I got up and started gathering my clothes. "I think I need to go."

"Wait. Don't leave."

"I think I should. I'm not in the right frame of mind right now to deal with this. I don't want anyone to get hurt."

He grabbed my arm. "It's too late for that, Teri. You made love to me tonight. Your body let me know that you wanted me, you needed me. I have never had a connection with anyone like that before," he said. For the first time, I saw something in his eyes I didn't like.

"I was *horny*, Sean. That's it!" I said, snatching my arm away. "What the hell is your problem?"

"Look, Teri. I wanted to try to free your mind, that's all. Let you know that you are much deeper than you or that piece of shit husband realize."

I hopped around as I tried to pull on my jeans.

"You have no idea," he said, shaking his head. "This is not how this is supposed to be."

"How this is supposed to be?" I repeated. "A month, Sean. You have known me for four weeks!"

"That doesn't matter. You have known me for the same amount of time and you just made love to me, Teri, without a condom."

I cringed when he said that. I really wanted to block out that part of the night. I had already tried to convince myself that I hadn't just done that, especially when I knew better.

It didn't take a rocket scientist to know that HIV and STDs were the real deal. My irresponsible decision would haunt me for a long time; longer than I could have ever imagined.

"I realize what I did, Sean. And it was irresponsible of both of us."

He sat on the bed, watching me get dressed with a towel draped across his lap. "Teri, I did what I did out of my feelings for you. Why did you do it?"

I grabbed my purse. "I have to go."

The ride to Renee's was excruciating. Gwinnett seemed like it was a world away. I replayed the night: the sound of the music, the softness of the dance dress, and how free I felt when I was dancing. It was bittersweet. I checked the message on my phone. It was Donovan. There was no way I was going to call him—not right now.

Sean was making himself out to be everything I wanted, or thought I wanted. He was everything that Donovan wasn't, or at least hadn't been during the past year. I had always heard about soul mates, but never believed in them. I thought I believed in that whole "'til death do us part" mess, but that was quickly becoming a long shot. Donovan had hurt me, and I had hurt him.

Our war should be over, but for some reason, I had the feeling it was just beginning.

Chapter Fifteen

Two more weeks passed and I found myself still staying with Renee.

I was actually closer to downtown and was able to spend time working on other things. I had even done some research on some dance classes at Georgia State, so all wasn't bad—or so I thought.

Sean and I had come to an understanding: I was not trying to become his replacement wife and, luckily for me, he had been in heavy rotation at the hospital, so his free time was scarce. He was averaging one day off and twenty-four hour shifts, so I was able to regroup after our raw sex episode.

I was in my room getting ready for work when I heard footsteps running down the hall toward my door.

"Teri! There is a tow truck outside hitching up your car!"

I tossed my makeup bag on the bed and ran down the steps.

A large black man in dingy blue coveralls and a dirty Atlanta Braves hat was writing something on a clipboard while his partner was hooking chains up under my car.

"Excuse me! What are you doing?" I shouted.

"We have orders to repossess this car."

"Repossess? This is *my* car and it was paid for with *cash*."

The huge tow truck sputtered and shook to life as it began pulling my car onto its flatbed. The huge man had to raise his voice over the noise.

"Sorry ,ma'am, but we have orders from the owner to pick it up."

My mind was racing.

The owner. What were they talking about?

The owner. I was the owner.

The owner. The car was brand new when I bought it.

The owner.

Then it hit me like a ton of bricks. Donovan was the owner.

The car was in his name; he paid for it. Not me. I ran back in the house and grabbed the phone. I dialed Donovan's work number so fast that I had to redial it twice because I kept hitting the wrong numbers.

He answered. My voiced echoed. "Take me off speaker phone, now!"

He snatched up the receiver. "Is this what it takes to get you to return my calls?"

"My car, Donovan? My fucking car! Donovan, what about my patients?"

"Not my problem. And it's the car I gave my *wife* for her birthday two years ago. You seem to have abandoned your wifely duties, so all bets are off!"

"I hate you!"

"No, you don't."

"You want me to come back home, to what?" I shouted. "You treated me like shit! You cheated on me!" I tried to keep an eye on the tow truck driver so I could see if he was leaving with my only mode of transportation, or if Ashton Kutcher was going to jump out of the bushes and start laughing.

"I know, and you will never know how sorry I am for doing that," he said. "I just want you to do what you promised you would do."

"What was that, Donovan?"

The anger left his voice. "Love me—be my wife."

I exhaled, regrouped. "I do love you."

"Then why?"

"I don't have an answer to that."

He let out sigh. "Hold on."

He put me on hold. My friend came to my side and asked if I was okay. I assured her I was, and she went back to the front door to watch the tow truck drivers.

I heard the truck die and my husband came back to the phone.

"What are you going to do, Teri?" he asked matter-of-factly. "I have the driver on the phone. If you agree to come home, he'll put the car back on the ground and go on about his day. If not, he's bringing it to me."

"Why are you doing this to me?"

"You did this to yourself."

"I hate you so much right now."

"Does it make you feel better to keep saying that? We both messed up. This isn't about me anymore; it's about us."

"Whatever."

"Oh, yeah, you don't want to hear that, do you? Probably because you are still sleeping with him."

"And if I am?"

"Don't play with me, Teri! I'll snap his bitch-ass neck!"

"Go to hell, Donovan!"

"You think I am playing with you, Teri? Try me."

"You know what, do what you have to do!"

I slammed the phone so hard it broke into two pieces. I heard the tow truck come back to life, snatching away my sanity. Renee came running in the living room.

"What is going on? Why are they taking the car?"

I sank down onto the couch and tried to fight the tears, but they came in waves, racking my body.

"Donovan . . . he is taking my car because I won't come back home."

She sat next to me and put her arm around me. "Damn, Teri. He is out of control! Go home!"

I looked at my friend. "I don't have a home anymore, Renee."

She grabbed me by the shoulders and held me tight.

"Yes, you do. That man doesn't want or need that car; he wants you. Don't you see that? He is the one who loves you—not Sean. Donovan loves you."

I got up and ran back upstairs. I heard the truck roaring down the street with my car safely chained to the back.

Damn what Renee was saying. Donovan was being vindictive and I wasn't trying to surrender to that—no matter what he did. I was tired of being something else for someone else.

"Teri!"

Renee was right behind me, trying to get me to listen, trying to tell me what she thought needed to be done.

"Renee, please. Not right now." I grabbed some tissue off the dresser and wiped my face.

"I am not trying to preach, and you know you can stay here as long as you want, but something has to be done about your marriage. Either go home or let that man go!"

"I know that, Renee," I said.

"I don't think you do. At what point are you and Donovan going to end this game you're playing with each other?"

"I am not playing any game."

"Yes, you are, Teri. What is Sean all about?"

"This has nothing to do with Sean. This is about my husband and our screwed up marriage."

"It takes two to be in a marriage, Teri. Maybe you need to step back and examine your own drama."

"Excuse me?"

She folded her arms across her chest. "Come on. In almost three years practicing, you never called in," she said.

"And?"

"And," she started, "you called in yesterday."

"So."

"Because you were with Sean."

"No, I called in because I needed some time to myself."

Renee shook her head.

Before I destroyed my friendship with her, I suggested that I should leave.

"Where are you going to stay? With Sean?"

"I don't know, Renee. Maybe."

"You can't stay with him, Teri. I don't trust him."

I looked at her. "You don't even know him."

"Hell, for that matter, neither do you! You know what, do what you want! If you are hell bent on destroying your life—hell—letting this *man* destroy your life then go ahead!"

She stormed out of the room, slamming the door behind her.

I stopped for a second, exhaled some negative and tried to suck in more positive than my lungs could hold. I tried to focus but couldn't.

I paced the small room. I thought about my master bedroom; thought about Sean's master bedroom. I picked up my cell and dialed Donovan's number, but hung up before it ever started to ring.

I continued to pace the carpet and thought about calling Sean. An hour later, I turned down Renee's offer of nourishment, but caved on her suggestion of tea. I sipped the hot, green liquid as I sat on the edge of change. I knew that nothing about my life was ever going to be the same. Nothing. Seven years of marriage had been trivialized, by both of us. I couldn't deny my feelings for Sean, no matter how juvenile they were, and I didn't think I should have to. Hell, a few weeks was nothing compared to what Donovan had done.

When I could no longer take Renee coming in and out of my room checking on me and offering me food, I took her car keys and headed into the office.

My one o'clock was already in my office waiting for me.

"I'm sorry it took me so long—noonday traffic," I said, hanging up my jacket

"That's okay. I just got here myself," Monica said with a weak smile.

I could tell Monica didn't care very much for herself. She oozed depression and loneliness. During our session, I couldn't help but disconnect. It was hard to focus as I listened to her try to explain her missteps in trying to find love and happiness. I couldn't help but wonder if this was God's way of sending me a message, using this woman to show me my own faults; how my husband could've possibly been tempted. So what? Was God trying to tell me this was my fault?

She continued, "He told me he loved me and when he told me, I believed him," she said.

"You believed him?" I asked, trying not to sound so unconvinced. "Even though you knew he was married."

"Yes, I did," she answered pitifully.

"Have you talked to him recently?"

"No. He won't take any of my calls."

"Why is that?"

"He's back with his wife."

My skin crawled with her statement.

I thought about Donovan casting Tracie to the side and returning home to me as if nothing happened. I swear this woman was my punishment—my constant reminder of how screwed up my life really was.

I called Sean after I got back to Renee's and told

him what happened with Donovan. I tried to downplay it, but my voice told the truth.

"Are you going to be okay?"

"I'll be fine."

His voice was low and loving. "You can come here."

I shook my head. "No, I can't."

"Why not? I know you are not still holding true to him. Not after what he did."

"It's more than that."

"Explain it to me."

"He's my husband."

"Look, I am not on rotation for the next two days. Give me two days, Teri."

I asked, "Why do you care so much?"

His voice changed to that of a lover.

"Teri."

"Yes."

"I'm coming to get you."

Thirty minutes later, I was sitting in Renee's living room, listening to her tell me how I was ruining my life and making a huge mistake. She paced the huge window, looking out and waiting for Sean. She was waiting to give him a piece of her mind, like a mother protecting her young. The only thing was, I wasn't a child. I didn't need protection.

Renee let out a sound somewhere between disgust and despair. "Teri, you know I am not happy about this. You can stay here. You don't have to go to Sean's place."

"I need to go, Renee."

I stood up and told her that I needed to work things out my way. I told her I would probably just have Sean take me to the Hilton downtown.

"I really just need a friend right now."

She hugged me. "Fine. But I think you are being selfish."

"Okay. That's your opinion, but why is that so bad? Being selfish for once?"

Renee shook her head, asked if I was sure, and then agreed not to lock onto Sean like an angry pit bull.

"Please don't tell Donovan where I am."

She slouched back into the couch. "That's not fair, Teri. This is your mess."

"Renee, would you please just do this for me and stop with the guilt trip?"

"I am not making you feel anything. Guilt comes from the inside. I can't make you feel anything you aren't already struggling with."

I was so sick of her preaching I could've choked her, but she was a true friend. She was just putting my shit under my nose and making me smell it.

Things had gotten complicated and feelings had grown out of situations that weren't supposed to exist. My husband had changed right before my eyes. I had changed right before my eyes.

"You're my sister, Teri. What happens to you, happens to me."

"Thank you."

"Why don't you take my car? That way you'll have the option of leaving that nut's house if you want."

I laughed. "He is not a nut. And you know your car wouldn't make it to Bankhead, let alone Dunwoody. It barely got me to work and back today."

She hit my leg and had to laugh at that. She hugged me and told me to be careful.

The doorbell rang. As I looked out the window, Renee peeked around me and saw his black Range Rover parked out front. She made a noise indicating that she was impressed.

She cracked a smile. "Hmm, a doctor, huh?"

I winked. "A cardiologist."

"Oh, he's a smart doctor." Her eyebrow raised.

She opened the door and did her best to be cordial to Sean. She even invited him into her home.

"Are you ready, Teri?"

"Yeah, let me get my bag from the dining room."

Just as I was about to grab my suitcase, my cell phone rang. It was home. I turned my phone off and shoved it into the side pocket of my suitcase on wheels. I felt a hand on my shoulder.

It was Sean.

"Let me get that."

I swallowed the lump in my throat and smiled at my Mr. Right Now. I let him carry my bag to his car as I hugged Renee and promised her that I would call her later.

The ride to his house was longer than usual. The Range Rover that once held our passion was uncomfortably cold.

I reached over and turned on the heat.

"Are you okay?" Sean asked.

I just nodded and kept looking out the window.

"Do you want to talk about it?"

"Not really."

"Do you need anything?"

I looked at him ready to snap and tell him to leave me alone. The care in his eyes stopped me from wounding this relationship as well. I told him I was okay. I just needed some sleep.

I tried to see myself divorced; dating, even dating Sean. Somehow, the image in my mind seemed fabricated and unrealistic. Donovan had always been there, but that didn't make it any better. I closed my eyes and said a little prayer.

I hoped the Lord still listened to the prayers of sinners like me.

Chapter Sixteen

I sat on Sean's couch and took a deep breath.

He had already taken my bags upstairs. I managed to get my cell out before he saw me. I turned it on; it made all kinds of beeps and dings, letting me know I had messages. There were both text and voicemail messages—twenty, to be exact—all from Donovan.

That made the tears flow fast and hard. I leaned forward, hiding my face in my hands, and let it out. Sean wrapped his arm around my shoulder and pulled me to him. His scent made my head swirl.

My husband was giving me a "get out of marriage free" card. I could leave now and start over, or I could check myself and try to make my marriage work.

"Do you want to talk?"

His voice broke my train of thought and added a sense of realism to my situation.

"No, I don't, and please stop asking me that. I just need to lie down."

He stood up and took my hand.

"I'll tell you what, why don't you stay in my guest room."

I reluctantly accepted his attempt at making this easy.

He said, "I promise I won't bother you." He walked toward the kitchen. "Do you want something to eat?"

"No."

I felt my phone vibrate. It was Donovan. Sean stopped in his tracks and looked back at me.

"Are you going to answer that?" he asked.

I looked at him. "I have to."

"No, you don't," he snapped.

"I don't need this right now, Sean." I walked out into the foyer and answered. "Yes."

"Where are you?"

"Why, Donovan? You told me to leave and you sent that truck for my car—"

"You slept with some other nigga! How is it that that point keeps getting overlooked?"

I shook my head. "Whatever."

"Where are you?"

"Somewhere where I'm wanted."

I heard glass breaking, and him swearing and yelling in Spanish.

"Damn it, Teri, you better not be with him! I swear—"

"Damn, it's real funny how all that understanding and love just went out the window, Donovan."

"Don't play with me," he said.

"You started this."

"And I guess you are going to try to finish it? Is that it, Teri?"

"You're damn right!"

"This is not a game. This is our life! What the hell has gotten into you?"

I slammed my phone closed.

"Teri."

Sean's voice sounded like it was a mile away. He walked me back to the sofa and handed me a cup of tea.

"Why don't you lie down?"

After taking a few sips of the chamomile tea, I followed him to the guest room. It was almost as big as his room. It had a huge private bathroom and balcony. Everything was white. From the sheer white, floor-length curtains to the fluffy white comforter on the huge canopy bed that I needed a step stool to climb into. Huge white scarves were draped over the top of the canopy, giving the room an Arabian feel. There were fresh white roses on a small breakfast table situated in front of the balcony doors. The room was very relaxing.

He handed me a towel and washcloth.

"I have some charts I am going to look over. Take your time."

"Okay."

He left me alone in my new room. I ran my fingers across the comforter. There were pillows all over the bed, and the Egyptian cotton sheets were very inviting. I was actually looking forward to sinking into the Tempur-Pedic mattress and getting a good night's sleep. I opened the glass doors that led out to the balcony and stepped out. The sun was losing its battle with the moon and the sky had taken on a beautiful hue of colors. I looked out toward downtown and found the thin strip of lights that illuminated I-85—lights that led the way home.

Before I climbed into bed, I took a long, hot shower. I was in desperate need of clarity and the hot shower was just the thing to give it to me. My head was hurting so badly, I popped some Aleve I found in the medicine cabinet. Once I was in bed, I turned on the television, but before I could settle on what to watch, I fell asleep.

I awoke dazed and confused. Once I realized where I was, I looked at the small clock on the nightstand. It was almost midnight. I pulled the robe Sean had given me over my shoulders and stepped into the hall.

The huge house was quiet—way too quiet. I walked down the hallway toward the double doors at the end. I ran my finger along the walls and couldn't help but smile at my own three-week search for the paint that I finally found to put in my own home.

I stopped at the door and listened to hear if Sean was awake. I could hear the sound of David Letterman's voice and then the music signifying the beginning of his famous "Top Ten List," which had something to do with Sarah Palin.

I pushed back the door. Sean was stretched out on his back and there were patients' folders on the bed next to him. Judging from the way he was breathing, I could tell he was asleep. I made my way across the large room to the edge of the bed and watched him sleep.

I sat on the edge of the bed and placed my hand on his chest. I felt his chest rise and fall with each breath. I ran my hand along his body. I felt the hardness of his chest the firmness of his arms.

I traced his face with my finger, and then ran it across his lips. I smiled at the thought of sleeping beauty.

The past couple months with him had been fun. I enjoyed our time together because I was able to be myself . . . or at least the person I thought I was supposed to be. I hated the thought of my fantasy coming to an end—of going back to my strained marriage, if I even still had one. But I knew I had to clean up my mess. I couldn't run forever.

I stood up and looked around his room. It was huge. The way the bed was situated, you could wake up and look directly out over the balcony to the swimming pool. I closed my eyes and imagined I lived here . . . had always lived here. I leaned down and got close to his face and inhaled his scent. I touched his lips with mine. That's when I felt his hand reach up and touch my face and I damn near jumped out of my skin. He opened his eyes, pulled my face to his, and kissed me.

"Can I have you?" he asked between kisses.

"Sean, you can't have me."

I felt his hand move up and slide my robe off my shoulders. I exhaled as pleasure took over, saturating the room. The pleasure wouldn't let me stop him from pulling my T-shirt over my head. He kissed up and down my back and hit a spot that made me squirm.

"This isn't right," I said.

"You want me to stop?"

"No."

He continued kissing my skin. He kissed me again and again, running his tongue along my neck, and stopping to nibble my ear. He laid me down, slid my panties off ,and kissed his way back up my body.

"You okay?"

I purred like a cat. "Ummm, I'm good."

"Are you still going back to the guest room?"

"Yes. In a few minutes."

He ran his tongue along the back of my knees. "You taste good."

Sean hit all the right spots. He made me chew on his pillow to keep from screaming as he ran his tongue along my inner thighs and let his tongue ease up and inside. He reached up and pulled the pillow from me.

"I want to hear you. Tell me how much you like it."

I was saying things and making sounds that were surprising to me, but it turned him on even more. The more I wiggled and moved, the more he worked it. I felt a wave start in my lower back; it rode my spine, causing my legs to tremble.

"Sean, what are you doing?"

"Loving you."

"Don't stop."

I loved the way he was listening to my body, giving me what I needed. He kissed his way up my body, not missing one spot on the way. He stopped at my breasts, and hung out there for a while, sending vibrations through me with every nibble and flick of his tongue.

I helped him out of his T-shirt, reached down into his shorts and found what he was offering.

He said. "Are you sure?"

"Yes."

I wanted him to hear me, hear what my insides were saying, and understand where I was coming

127

from. I needed him to take me where I was trying to go, and then I wanted us to retrace our steps. I let out a low groan as he broke skin, entering me slowly and deliberately. He pulled out and his gaze met mine as he eased back in slowly, in and out. He held that rhythm until my orgasm rose from the soles of my feet, shaking my legs, and making me scream out his name. I felt him twitching inside, an extension of my own orgasm.

He rolled off of me, both of us trying to catch our breath. A few minutes later, I heard water running, then he was cleaning me with a warm, wet towel. I reached down and put my hand over his.

"I think I can handle this."

He smiled. "No problem."

I cleaned up and put the towel in his hamper.

Sleep came down on me before I realized it. I yawned, then reached for my balled-up T-shirt and panties and pulled them both on.

"Are you leaving me?" he asked.

"Should I?"

"No. I want you here when I wake up."

He hugged me close to him. I felt his body get heavy, then I heard his breathing change, slow down. I could barely keep my eyes open.

"I have to go back to my husband, Sean."

I tried to explain, apologize even but my mouth was heavy, and I could no longer keep my eyes open.

He pulled me close. "I can't let you do that."

Chapter Seventeen

I woke to the most annoying sound.

It made me jump and damn near fall out of the bed. Sean grabbed my arm to keep me from hitting the floor head first.

"Sorry about that."

He reached over and turned off his alarm. I looked at the clock; it was six-thirty. I let out a groan and pulled the blanket over my head.

He said, "I forgot to turn it off. Working these twenty-four-hours days got me twisted."

I snuggled up to him. It was too early. I didn't even know what six A.M. looked like, and had no desire of getting to know it. The week I had been with him so far was nice. I had to admit I enjoyed not dealing with arguments and tension almost daily.

I felt him slide out of bed.

"Where are you going?"

"Nature calls."

I was asleep before the toilet flushed.

Later that morning, Sean made us pancakes and bacon. We were sitting at his kitchen table eating when his phone rang.

He looked at me and I shrugged.

He said, "At least it isn't a pager."

"True."

He went into the other room. I heard him talking, and then his voice got so low for a moment I couldn't hear anything but the sound of the refrigerator. Then I heard him fussing, telling someone that they couldn't control what was happening.

I took that opportunity to check my cell. When I turned it on, it quickly sprang to life with five new messages. Three messages were from Donovan, full of more threats, less promises. One was a hang-up, and the other was Renee.

"Teri, call me. Donovan is acting real weird. I tried to tell him you weren't here, that you were in a hotel, which you better be, but he wasn't buying it." She paused like she was contemplating what to do next. "Call me back."

My line beeped. I looked at the display. It was work. Without thinking, I answered.

"Yes."

"Teri, this is Martin. I was hoping to meet with you today."

"I have a ten o'clock. Can we say noon?"

"Make it eleven-thirty."

Click!

I shook my head and played through all the messages from Donovan. I deleted some without listening, but I couldn't help but listen to others. He sounded hurt, and part of me wanted to run to him and jump into his arms and make all of our problems go away. Yet, the part of me that wasn't happy was too strong, and it had taken over.

I showered and dug around in my suitcase to find something to wear. It was almost nine, and I needed to rent a car to get to work.

Sean stood in the door watching me. "Where are you going?"

"I gotta go. I have a patient at ten and a meeting at eleven-thirty."

He smiled. "I can see why your husband is craving you. You're a busy woman."

I chuckled as I pulled my suit out of my garment bag.

"I am going to call and see if I can't get someone to bring me a rental. Isn't there a rental company that does that? Enterprise, right?"

He shook his head, stepped into the room. "Don't do that. Just take my car."

"Your Range Rover?"

"No, my car. I have a car in the garage."

"Are you sure?"

"Yes."

"Okay. I will be back as soon as I am finished."

He winked. "Take your time. I know where to find you."

I smiled. "Of course you do."

Sean gave me the keys to his Mercedes CLK and told me it was mine if I wanted it, for as long as I needed it. When I made it to work, people in the office were standing around chatting. A few spoke, but most of them acted as if they were scared to speak.

"Dr. McCall," Eva started, "you have a message from someone named Darienne." I took the pink paper with the name and number scribbled on it and kept moving. I tossed the message in my inbox, sat behind my desk, and pulled up my e-mails while I sifted through the mountain of paper that was on my desk. A tap on my door caused me to look up at Harrison and smile.

"Hey, you made it."

"Yes. I was a little under the weather."

"Glad you are back though. We missed you yesterday."

I just smiled and continued to prepare for my ten o'clock session. He took my hint and walked away and I was glad. I wasn't trying to have small talk. I didn't like the tone in Dr. Lee's voice, and I was anxious to see what it was all about.

After my first session of the day was over later that morning, I checked my clock. It was 11:30. I stood up, took a deep breath, and made my way toward the huge office at the end of the hall.

His door was open. I tapped lightly and pushed it back. Dr. Lee perked up when he saw me.

"Hello, Teri. Please close the door and come in."

I took a seat in the chair across from him and tried to suppress my nervousness, but my stomach was bubbling like a pot of gumbo.

"What did you need to see me about?" I asked, ready to let the shoe fall and get it over with.

He slid an envelope toward me. I swallowed and tried to avoid throwing up as I touched it and began to open it.

"This was delivered to me this morning." He stood up and walked around his desk as he continued his speech. "This practice prides itself on family and values, Teri. Can you explain those?"

I slid the black and white pictures from inside the envelope. I prayed they were pictures of me at last year's Christmas party. I had had a little too much to drink and ended up dancing on the piano with Sylvia, the girl who worked in the mailroom.

My prayer wasn't answered. I found myself holding the same pictures that my husband had shoved in my face. Pictures of me, having sex with a man who was not my husband. Luckily, whoever sent them had written *ADULTERER* in huge red letters, and the word covered most of my naked body.

He asked, "Is there anything you want to talk about, Teri? What is going on?"

I shoved the pictures back in the envelope and stood up. If I was going down, I was going to do it with dignity.

"I–I'm very sorry, Dr. Lee."

He held up his hands. "No apologies. I just want

to make sure that you are going to be okay with this new promotion."

He continued, "Let's put things on hold. Let you get yourself together, and then we will revisit the promotion in a little while to see where we are."

All I could to was thank him and agree. After assuring the man that I had everything under control, apologizing, and doing everything short of groveling, I left his office. I brushed past Eva, and stormed back into my office, knocking my inbox on the floor in the process. I stooped down and started scooping up the pile of papers and slamming them on top of my already messy desk.

I was so caught up in my own anger that I didn't hear anyone come in. But the voice was all too familiar, and so was the Latino accent.

"Would you like some help?"

"Donovan, what are you doing here?" I asked without turning around.

"This was the only way I could pin you down."

I stood up and looked at him before continuing to pick up what was left of the papers.

"What do you want, Donovan?"

He pushed the door to my office closed. The soft click of the door catching made my heart skip a beat. I slid into the chair behind my desk.

"Don't be like that, Teri. I came here to talk to you."

Although I tried not to show it, I missed him. I missed the sound of his voice, and even his scent.

He was looking damn good dressed in a dark blue Hugo Boss suit, wearing a tie I bought him not too long ago from Saks. His hair was wavy, not as curly as it usually was; he must've combed gel through it instead of letting it air dry. It wasn't hard to see what that bitch saw in him. Today his African-American genes were more prevalent, his skin tone was darker than usual, and his eyes were a beautiful deep shade of brown.

133

"It took me having an affair for you to finally get it, Donovan?" I said, trying to fix the mess I made. I buried the envelope with the pictures under a stack of files.

"What difference does it make? I'm here now and I'm trying to fix things." He sighed and walked over to the window. I continued to fidget with the papers in front of me. Having him here in my space made things real. I hadn't seen him since the night of the argument, and a few more nights wouldn't have hurt.

"I want you to come home, Teresa."

"What if I am not ready for that?"

He spun around. "Why wouldn't you be ready to come home to your husband?"

"Donovan, a lot has happened—things that need to be dealt with—addressed."

He looked at me. "You already know that I ended mine. Are you prepared to do the same?"

I rubbed my hand across my forehead. "It's not that."

"Then what is it?"

"It's me."

He took a step toward me, causing me to flinch and back away.

A confused look spread across his face. "What? You scared of me now?"

He bit his bottom lip and cut his eyes to the door then back to me.

He asked, "How did you get to work today?"

"Excuse me?"

"You heard me." He repeated, "How have you been getting to work, Teri?"

His tone was firm and suspicious, making me uncomfortable because I knew what the answer was.

"Why are you so concerned about my transportation? You weren't worried when you snatched my car away last week."

"I did that to get your attention, Teri. You weren't listening to me. And after I got those pictures . . . "

His voice trailed off. He swallowed his hurt; I kept mine to myself. He looked at me. Time stood still. There were no loud noises coming from the hall, no music pumping through the radio on my book shelf. It was just me and him—husband and wife.

"I need time, Donovan." I finally said.

"Time for what, Teri? Where are you sleeping?"

"In a hotel."

"Which one?"

"Why?"

"Just answer the question, Teri!"

"Donovan, I told you, I need some time to work through this. Why won't you give me time?"

"How much time?"

"I don't know," I whispered.

He walked up to me and got so close I could count the hairs in his goatee. I braced myself on the edge of the desk as he bent down and got in my face.

"If I find out you are still messing with him, I am going to hurt him . . . then I'm coming after you. That's a promise. You are MY wife. Remember that."

I pressed myself closer to my desk. "That's crazy."

"You think so? Try me."

Before the first tear rolled down my cheek, he was gone. I started to run after him, but too much had happened; not only on his part, but on mine. Things couldn't just be swept under the rug and forgotten.

I pulled the envelope out from its hiding place, and hit the switch on my paper shredder. I fed the envelope into it without opening it again. I didn't need to see my own mess again.

I remembered hearing someone once say, "The grass is greener on the other side, until you have to mow it."

That was so true.

Almost two hours after Donovan left, I was still in my office gathering my things when the phone rang. Reluctantly, I answered, "Dr. McCall."

For a second, no one said anything. There was silence on the line. Then, finally, a weird voice came over the line.

"You took my life; now I'm about to take yours."

"Who is this?"

"Don't worry about that. You need to be more concerned with your husband. Do you know where he is? I do!"

The voice on the other side was angry, but I couldn't make it out.

"Who is this?"

Click!

I slammed the phone down then picked it up and quickly dialed Donovan's cell.

No answer. I left him a message and told him to call me as soon as he could. I ran my fingers through my hair and thought about riding to Cobb County. Then I changed my mind. There was no way I could explain driving another man's car to my own house.

"Dammit!" I said out loud to no one.

I grabbed my purse and headed down to the parking deck. My mind was racing. I figured that if I could switch cars with Renee, then I could go by my house and check on Donovan.

It was abnormally cold in the parking garage as the wind cut through the deck making it angry as it whipped around my body. I hugged my purse to my body and picked up my pace as I headed toward Sean's car. I knew now more than ever that I had to find Donovan and make this right.

I heard footsteps behind me, causing me to stop and spin around.

No one was there. I told myself to stop imagining things and continued toward the car. I made sure the keys were in my hand and ran my finger along the panic button on the small remote to make sure I knew where it was. Again, I heard the footsteps.

At that point, I was damn near running. I had parked the car as far from the door as I could because I didn't want anyone to see me in it, but now I wanted to get to the car as quickly as possible.

It was too late.

The blow to the head caused me to fall to the cold concrete right at the door to the car.

I managed to hit the panic button before the next blow came, knocking me out cold.

Chapter Eighteen

"Doctor Allen, please dial extension 1763. Doctor Allen, please dial extension 1763."

A monotone voice came screaming into my psyche as I tried to open my eyes. I couldn't seem to focus and my mouth felt like it was full of cotton. I tried to swallow, but there was nothing there to swallow. My head was pounding like someone was using it as a bass drum.

A voice told me to close my eyes and rest.

So I did.

I don't know how much time passed before I woke up the second time. I opened my eyes and looked around. I was in the hospital, but I didn't know which one. A nurse whose name tag said JACQUI was taking my blood pressure. The blood pressure cuff ripped into the silence of the room as she took it off making me jump. She was smiling at me.

"Well, hello there," she said, smoothing down my hair.

Jacqui looked to be in her mid-forties. She had shoulder length blonde hair, and her brown eyes were deep set behind her designer-framed glasses. Her small hands were warm; most nurses I had dealt with had ice cubes for hands. The slipcover on her stethoscope was covered with kittens.

I tried to ask her what was going on, but my

throat was too dry. I couldn't get the words out, so I started coughing.

"Shhh, don't talk," she said. "I am going to call your doctor."

Thankfully, before she left, she held a cup of water to my lips so I could take a sip. My mind was screaming, jumping up and down, and trying to figure out what was going on. I tried to move my arm and winced from the pain that shot through it. My whole body throbbed with pain.

For the first time, I noticed a figure asleep in the small pull-out chair in the corner.

It was Renee.

I looked up at the television hanging in the corner. It was on *CNN Headline News*. The tiny clock at the bottom of the screen said 3:59 A.M. (PST), which meant it was barely seven A.M. here.

I looked toward the window and watched daylight win its battle with darkness. The sun started to make its way over the horizon, shining a light on Renee that caused her to stir and stretch. She yawned and looked at me.

"Girl, am I glad to see you."

I tried to talk, but it got caught in my throat. I coughed it out and asked her what was going on. I sounded more like an 80-year-old chain smoker than myself. "Where am I? Where's Donovan?"

"You don't remember what happened?"

I shook my head. "I was walking to my car, trying to get to Donovan. Someone called me and threatened him. That's the last thing I remember."

She looked at me, confused. "Somebody attacked you in the parking deck. Why were you worried about Donovan? Who would want to hurt him?"

That made me remember the blow to my head. I reached up and felt the bandage on the back of my head and told her about the phone call. "Did anyone see who it was?"

"No. They are trying to check the cameras, but you know how that is."

I took a deep breath. My side was sore. I winced and reached up to touch it. "Who found me?"

"When the car alarm went off, the security guard ran his fat behind upstairs. He said he scared off whoever it was."

I tried to sit up. "I need to find Donovan and make sure he's okay."

"I couldn't get in touch with him. The hospital and I tried the numbers in your cell under recent calls. I have been trying to call him all night. Do you know where he is?"

"No," I answered, my gut twisted with worry. That phone call haunted me more than I wanted to admit.

"What about—"

She finished my sentence. "Sean?"

"Yes."

"He's doing rounds. He was here this morning while you were asleep."

That bit of information let me know I was at Crawford Long, which made my head really hurt. I did not need him and Donovan bumping heads and disturbing all these sick folk.

"What did the doctor say?" I asked.

"Bump on the head, bruised ribs, but you'll live."

I rolled my eyes. "Lucky me."

"How long have I been in here?"

"Just a day."

"What is today?" I asked, flipping the channel, trying to find something that would let me know.

"Saturday."

I reached up and rubbed my neck.

She held up the paper. I was on the front page: DOCTOR ATTACKED IN PARKING GARAGE. NO SUSPECTS. "You are a bona fide celeb."

I laughed. "They could've used a picture."

My friend propped herself on the edge of my hospital bed and I told her what happened in my office between Donovan and me.

"And you're surprised?" she asked.

"Yes. I can't believe what this has turned into."

"I can't see why you're surprised. What about your doctor friend? Are you sure he has nothing to do with your lack of concern for your marriage?"

I looked at her and tried to let her know I didn't want to go there, but she kept on.

She said, "Think about it, Teri. Before Sean, it was just you and Donovan, working through a situation. Now, you aren't sure if you want to work through that situation *and* you are sleeping with another man."

"That is not the point."

"Yes, it is the point."

I closed my eyes and hoped she would just leave. I didn't want to argue with her or try to justify my feelings for Sean, especially not now.

A tap on the door saved me and saved her from getting cussed out. A tall, white doctor walked in holding a clipboard. He smiled at me then wrote something down on his paper.

"Good morning, Dr. McCall. How are you feeling?"

"Like I have been run over by a truck."

He chuckled. "Yeah, you took quite a blow to the head. I am Dr. Delgado. I am doing rounds for Dr. Lawson. He is going to be happy to know that you're awake."

He started pressing on parts of my body, having me squeeze his finger, and lifting my limbs and laying them down. He shined a light in my eyes, felt around the bandage on my head, and then checked my throat.

He continued to scribble on his clipboard. "I am going to give you a few prescriptions. One for pain, the other is an antibiotic. I want you to take the pain pills only if you need them. Otherwise, Motrin will be okay. You can take up to three Motrin at a time. That's about six hundred milligrams."

He continued telling me about my medicine, how the strong stuff would make me sleepy, and the antibiotic was just a precaution.

He flipped through my chart, humming to himself. Suddenly, his personal cantata stopped.

I asked, "What's wrong?"

"I didn't see this," he said, flipping through more pages then looking at me. "You're pregnant."

I felt like I had been punched in the stomach. The room started spinning. Renee grabbed my hand and I squeezed hers.

"Excuse me?"

"Dr. Lawson has noted here that your blood showed elevated levels of HCG, indicative of pregnancy. You didn't know, Dr. McCall?"

"Does it look like she knew?" Renee snapped.

"I'm sorry, Dr. Delgado." I shot Renee a look telling her to shut up. "No, I didn't know. How far along?"

"It doesn't say. You would have to have an ultrasound to determine exactly how far into the pregnancy you actually are."

Visions of sex with Sean over the past month and a half flashed through my mind. I tried to blink them back and make them go away. It was made worse when I heard the knock on the door.

Renee opened the door and in walked Sean, adding more stress to my moment. He was in scrubs and his lab coat. He and Dr. Delgado looked like bookends. He looked at me and smiled, then spoke to Dr. Delgado.

"Hey there, Dr. Morris." He extended his hand. "What brings the all powerful cardiologist down here?"

"I was here checking on a patient whose pacemaker I put in yesterday." He laughed. "Thought I would come by and check on my friend."

"Oh, Dr. McCall is a friend of yours? Well, she is going to be just fine."

Dr. Delgado touched my leg assured me that I would be discharged by tomorrow and left.

Renee sat in the corner, speechless. She started flipping channels, trying to act like she didn't see Sean. I tried to act like I hadn't gotten the news, but subconsciously, my hand covered my belly.

"Hi," I said as he made his way toward my bed.

"How are you feeling?"

"Not bad. Really sore."

He turned his attention to Renee. "If you want to go home and get some rest, you can. I am off soon. I can stay with her."

Renee shot him a look. "That's okay. I'm fine. Besides, what if her *husband* shows up, Dr. Slick Dick?"

Sean's eyes flashed anger, and I could tell he was about to say something that was going to cause a fight that I wasn't in the mood for.

"Renee!" I said.

"Teri, this is ridiculous!" She continued, "Seriously, what if Donovan shows up?"

Sean tilted his head and looked at me. "Oh yeah, where is your husband?"

My thoughts went to the phone call I had gotten just before I ended up here, and I felt sick.

"I don't know," I said.

Sean just shook his head. "Where is your chart?" he asked.

My mind went to the pregnancy results, and I didn't need that stress. I was glad when I realized that the doctor had taken it.

"Why?"

"I just want to see what medicines they have you on."

"Motrin."

"You want something stronger?"

I shook my head. "No, I'll be okay."

Renee rolled her eyes and returned to her seat. A wave of queasiness rolled through me. I desperately needed the past two months to disappear quicker than a crack head when the police showed up.

"Okay, well, I am gonna finish my rounds. I'll be back later." He looked at Renee, who continued to act as if he weren't even in the room.

I managed to fall asleep and when I woke up, Renee was gone and Sean was asleep in her spot. The channel had been changed from CNN to ESPN. I shook my head and imagined Donovan somewhere watching the same thing.

I glanced at the window next to him. The sun had long gone home for the day. I could see the tops of the buildings that lit up downtown and wondered what place my husband had in that darkness. Darkness brought out the worst in people; it made them do things they were ashamed of at the crack of dawn.

I reached down and touched my belly. I thought about the secret it held. I closed my eyes and imagined it big and round; Donovan rubbing it, smiling, and finally getting what he always wanted.

"You okay?"

Sean's groggy voice broke me out of my trance. I looked toward him. He looked tired and worn—like a man who had sat watch by his lover all night. I felt sorry for him. I felt badly for dragging him into my messed up life.

"I'm fine, really. I really just need to talk to my husband," I said.

"You can't be serious," he said.

I nodded slowly. "Yes, I am, Sean. This is getting out of control."

Anger spread across his face. "I'm not leaving without you."

"Sean, he's my husband. I have to talk to him."

His eyes were wild with anger. "Are you going back to him?"

I managed to sit up a little more in the bed. "What do you want from me, Sean?"

"I want you, Teri."

"I'm *married*, Sean. This whole mess should've never gotten started in the first place."

He began to pace the small room. "I'm warning you, don't do this."

"Excuse you! Warning me?"

He shoved his hands in his pockets and looked at me. I would have given anything to be able to go back in time and make whatever went wrong right . . . with me, with Donovan, whatever it took.

"I would hate for anything to happen to you or your husband, Teri."

"What is that supposed to mean?"

Without speaking, he grabbed his keys off the table and opened the door and disappeared, taking with him my sense of security and a little bit of my sanity.

I reached over and grabbed the phone. I dialed Donovan's cell and got no answer. Same thing happened when I tried the house. I sank back into the bed, changed the channel back to CNN, and turned it up. I listened to the anchor talk about some train crash out west and before I knew it, I drifted off to sleep.

I was dreaming about Donovan. We were happy, Tracie didn't exist, and things were the way they were meant to be. We were cuddling in bed, watching television, kissing and laughing like teenagers.

I opened my eyes and looked up into the eyes of Donovan. He was standing over me, watching me sleep. His eyes were bloodshot, and his hair was flat, like he had just woken up.

"Are you okay?" he asked.

"I'm fine. Are you okay?"

"Yes, I'm fine."

He touched my leg and asked what happened.

"Somebody attacked me in the parking deck at work." I blew out some air. "Where were you, Donovan? Renee tried to call you. Where were you?"

"I was at the office."

"Last night?"

He pushed the door closed, attempting to contain our argument within the four walls.

"Yes, last night. Teri, I don't want to go home if you're not there. I have been staying at the Hilton near the office."

That statement stopped my argument and made me feel a small twinge of sympathy for him.

"Why haven't you been answering your cell phone?"

"When I saw Renee's number, I didn't want to be bothered. I thought it was going to turn into another argument—so I didn't answer."

"How did you know I was here?"

"Renee left a message at home. So I came down here," he said.

I shifted in the bed and tried to get more comfortable. "So what? I guess you are here to drag me home kicking and screaming?"

He let out a sound of disgust. "No, Teri. I am here to check on my wife."

"I got a phone call before I left the office the other night."

"From?"

"I don't know, but whoever it is—they're watching you. They're watching both of us."

He shook his head and let out a hard sigh. "This has gotten way out of control, Teri. You need to come home." His eyes were loving and his tone was genuine, making me want to leap into his arms and tell him it was okay . . . but it was too late. Things would never be the same between us again. He sat on the edge of the bed, the same spot where Sean had sat a while before. He touched my hand; I pulled away. I rubbed my stomach. I wanted to tell him, but knew that would just make things worse.

"I don't know how much longer I can handle this little phase you're going through, Teri."

"That's what you think this is? A phase?"

"It's like all the plans we had, you just abandoned them to chase after whatever it is you're chasing."

"I am not chasing anything."

"Then what are you running from?"

I shook my head and rubbed the side of my face. He was making this harder than it had to be right now.

"I am not running from anything."

"Yes, you are, Teri. Why don't you admit it? What are you scared of? It's just me. The same man who has loved you from the first day he saw you. The man who wants nothing more than to start a family with you."

I closed my eyes for a second and tried to see things from his point of view. I realized he just wanted a wife. I was a wife, but I just wasn't sure I wanted to be one anymore. Too many lies had been told, too much had happened. I didn't even know who I was.

Donovan paced the floor, wearing a path in the floor between my bed and the window. He stopped at the window and looked out. Something held his attention long enough for me to catch a glimpse of Sean through the small window in the door to my room. Sean looked at me then to Donovan, anger written all over his face. I could tell he wanted to come in and start something, but my eyes begged him not to.

He disappeared from the small window, and then I turned my attention back to Donovan.

"Donovan, go home, get some sleep. I will be out of here in the morning."

147

"But you're not coming home."

"I don't know what I am going to do."

At that moment, Renee walked in fueled with attitude. She got up in Donovan's face and proceeded to tell him how pissed off she was at him for not calling her back. He shoved his hands in his pants pockets and let her rant and rave. "Renee, please," I said. I was tired, hungry, and I wanted to go back to sleep. I didn't need them in here cussing each other out.

"No, Teri. He needs to get it together and stop acting like a baby." She looked from him to me. "Both of you do! What is *wrong* with you two? You both are just going to stand by and let your marriage dissolve like this?"

He sighed, shook his head, and walked toward the door. "Teri, I am going home. You need to figure out what it is you want, or I won't be there when you get there."

He left before I could respond; left before he could hear Renee call him an asshole.

"Renee, don't do that. He is still my husband."

"Well, that's a shock!" she said. "That's the first smart thing you've said in weeks!"

I knew Renee was right. I had feelings for Sean, but the feelings for my husband ran deeper.

Yet, if I was carrying Sean's baby, that damn sure changed everything.

Chapter Nineteen

I checked into the Georgian Terrace Hotel downtown after being discharged.

Renee was pissed at me, Donovan was too much for me, and Sean was nutty. I just needed to be by myself for a little while. I couldn't deal with anyone else's drama, so there was no way I was going to work.

Dr. Lee told me to take as much time as I needed, and that he would make sure to take care of my patients. I warned him about Mr. Wendell and told him to be expecting a visit and a souvenir from the circus.

Two weeks later, I drove up Peachtree Street to a doctor I was referred to when they discharged me from the hospital. Dr. Lunsford was an OB/GYN who came highly recommended. I tried to swallow the fear that had settled in my throat trying to pretend I belonged in the small waiting room with the other pregnant-bellied mothers. But I knew I didn't belong. I was carrying another man's baby, while my husband sat at home waiting for me to decide if I wanted to stay married to him.

The examination room seemed to get smaller and smaller the longer I had to wait. I read the poster on the wall about a hundred times: BREAST MILK IS BEST! The caption was below the picture of a smiling mother and a nursing infant. I couldn't see why she was so happy about having something attached to her damn breast.

I heard a small tap on the door, and then Dr. Lunsford came in. She was a tall woman, with a soft face and calming demeanor. She smiled and shook my hand.

"Hello, Dr. McCall," she said. "I'm Dr. Lunsford." She looked through my chart, said a couple "uh-huhs" and "okays" before laying it on the counter. "Is this your first pregnancy?"

I shook my head. "I had a miscarriage about a year and a half ago."

She instructed me to lie down on the short examination table, and then buzzed for a nurse. A few seconds later, a shorter lady wearing a bright pink scrub shirt came in. She also smiled when she saw me. I couldn't figure out what the hell everyone was so damn happy about.

"I am going to manually check your cervix to make sure it's doing what it's supposed to."

She pulled on a pair of those latex gloves. I wanted to vomit. If my cervix hadn't done its job, I wouldn't be in this mess.

During her exam, I thought about my first pregnancy and how happy we were. Donovan called just about everybody he knew and a few people he randomly picked out of the phone book, just to tell them. I was upset at first, but I grew to be happy. I was trying to get my career going, trying to finally enjoy life for once, and bam, I got pregnant. But once my belly started to grow and I felt those first flutters, I couldn't have been happier. This time, I felt nothing. I was numb . . . the news hadn't sunk in yet.

The nurse said, "Okay, you can sit up now."

I slid back, tried to keep the small gown from showing off my goodies, and repositioned the paper wrap they gave me to throw over my legs.

The doctor jotted down some notes then turned to me. "Okay," she breathed. "Judging from your paper-work and the size of your uterus, you are right at about six weeks. The nurse is going to get the ultrasound machine and we are going to make sure. Have you been taking vitamins?"

"I just found out. I am still in shock."

She leaned against the small counter. Her tone changed. She went from congratulatory to inquisitive. "Do you plan on going through with the pregnancy?"

"I . . . I guess so," I stammered. "I hadn't really thought about it."

She looked at me with that look—the look disappointed parents give irresponsible teens when they pop up pregnant. It made me uneasy; made my face hot.

Just then, the nurse rolled in what looked like a television and a computer all rolled up into one. She instructed me to lie back, while the doctor tapped away on the small keyboard on the machine.

The nurse squirted some warm jelly on my stomach then ran the wand over my stomach. "If I can't get a reading this way, we may have to do this internally."

"Internally?" I asked. I had been poked enough.

"Yes. I will use a probe to take a look from another angle." She continued to roll the sticky wand around and sucked her teeth. "Yup, I am going to have to do it the other way."

She squirted some jelly on a long probe that looked like a huge vibrator, then covered the end with a condom. I giggled.

"Hey, somebody's gotta use them, right?" she said.

That shut down my private joke, especially since I knew better. A condom could've prevented this whole mess.

She began her internal probe; it felt weird and was more than a little uncomfortable. Just when I was about to jump up and tell her where to stick that damn wand, she turned the screen so I could see it.

There it was for me in black and white: the tiniest little blip I had ever seen. It looked more like a bean with fluid around it. I quickly realized it was so much more when I saw the flickering of the tiny heart beating. So much more.

Chapter Twenty

After leaving the doctor's office, I made my way back to the hotel.

Once I got settled, I called Renee. She answered on the first ring, like she was waiting for me to call. She immediately started in with the questions.

"What are you going to do, Teri?"

"I don't know, Renee."

"Have told Donovan yet?"

"No. He doesn't even know I went to the doctor."

She made a sound that let me know she didn't agree. Renee said, "So, exactly how long do you plan on keeping this up?"

"What do you expect me to do?"

"Maybe grow up and stop acting like a lovesick teenager."

"That's not fair, Renee."

"What you're doing is not fair. I don't know what your agenda is, but you need to get it together."

"I don't have an agenda."

"I don't understand what there is to think about. You need to let him know," she said.

I ran my fingers across my abdomen and tried to imagine what the tiny person would look like.

I said, "I will let him know, Renee. In my own time."

"When? When you are panting and pushing?"

I laughed. "No. Definitely not."

"Are you going to have it?"

That question had been rolling around in my head since I left Dr. Lunsford's office, but I had been dodging it like a big dog. She had given me the name and number of a clinic downtown. She said it was just to give me options.

"Why would you ask me that?"

"Because I know you."

"Renee," I sighed, "I don't know what I am going to do."

I looked down at my wedding rings and thought about how this was going to shatter my marriage beyond repair. My heart ached as I looked around the lifeless hotel room.

"Hold on."

"Who is that?"

"Derrick." She let out a sigh. "He is digging around for luggage. He is being deployed next week."

"To where?"

"Germany, remember?"

I had totally forgotten about Derrick leaving. I was so caught up in my own world. She hollered out, told him she was in the bedroom, and then asked him to leave his boots in the garage. "Those things stink up the house like you wouldn't believe."

A moment later, I heard her husband's voice, asking if she was hungry and where Christopher was. She told him Christopher was with her mother. Then I heard giggles and kisses. I rolled my eyes and wished she would get back to me and my problems.

"Teri?"

"I'm here."

"How long are you going to spend money on that room? You know you can come here. I am going to be here all by myself when Derrick leaves."

"I don't know. I may check out tomorrow."

"Come on over here. I will put on a pot of tea and we can come up with a solution to this situation."

I smiled at my friend's attempt to mother me. She was a good friend. I loved her for her honesty just as much as it got on my nerves.

"I'll see," I said. "I can't live off of you."

"You're right, you can't, but you can stay here."

"Shut up."

"A'ight, let me go," she said. "I need to help Derrick pack."

I rolled my neck and tried to accept that I wasn't top on her list of priorities.

I said, "Okay."

"You want to meet for lunch tomorrow?"

"I'll let you know."

Food was the farthest from my mind. My headache reminded me every second of the mess I was in. I couldn't shake the image of my husband and the past we shared, but I couldn't help but look to the future.

"Teri?"

"Yes."

"Go get something to eat and call me later."

"Okay."

"No matter what you decide, I will be there for you."

"Thanks."

"And don't panic. It's going to be okay."

"If you say so."

"I do, so it will."

We laughed. It was a forced laugh because we both knew that wasn't the truth.

I managed to get a nap and take a bubble bath before the sun went down. I couldn't help but continue to touch my stomach. The image of that little tiny life in there had gotten to me, forcing me to put things into perspective. No matter what had happened, there was no way I could stay married to Donovan being pregnant with another man's child.

Donovan wanted nothing more than for us to have a baby and make a family, then I go and get pregnant by another man. I had to shake my head at that one.

I picked up the phone, dialed room service, and ordered a burger and fries before calling Sean. He wasn't real happy about me leaving his house after I left the hospital, but I couldn't go back there. I needed neutral ground. He did agree to let me keep the car though, so at least I could get around.

"Are you okay, Miss Lady?"

"I'm fine. Waiting for room service."

"I can bring you something."

That was his way of working his way into my room. I told him no, that room service would be just fine.

"Sean, I have so many things I need to work out right now."

"Did you know that Donovan was coming to the hospital?" he asked.

"I figured that he would. He is my husband."

"Did you call him, or did Renee?"

"Renee, but what difference does it make? He is my husband, Sean."

"I know that, Teri, but he doesn't love you like I do."

"You don't even know me, Sean. How can you say you love me?"

"Teri, I have loved you since the first time I saw you."

"Don't do this, Sean."

"Why not? It's the truth."

I let out a sigh. "I can't just jump out of a marriage and move in with you."

"I am not asking you to do that, but I am asking for a chance to make you happy."

I looked around the room. It seemed smaller. I reached up, scratched my face, and rubbed my temple. I shouldn't have called him.

"Sean, I need to get some sleep. I will call you back in the morning."

"I want you to come back, Teri. You don't need to be in that hotel room by yourself."

"I am a big girl, Sean, I think I can manage."

"At least tell me where you are."

"I am downtown, Sean."

I touched my stomach and thought about Donovan.

He said, "I miss you, Teri. I want you in bed with me."

His baritone was hypnotizing causing the heart between my legs to thump, getting my attention.

"Is that right?"

"Yes. I want to make love to you."

I chewed my bottom lip, almost told him about the baby growing inside of me. I thought of him coming home from the hospital, bringing me whatever my latest craving was, laughing when I ate it all and offering to get me more. I imagined him rubbing my feet and telling me how beautiful I was as my belly swelled. I imagined rushing to the hospital, me panting and trying to remember my Lamaze breathing, him panicking and getting us lost. Then him having no problem finding his way home when it came time to drive us all back from the hospital. The only problem with the image was that the man in it wasn't Sean.

It was Donovan.

"Teri."

"Yes."

"Please, let me come get you."

"Sean, this is too much for me."

His let out an agitated sigh.

I had run from so many things in my life; I never expected happiness to be one of them, but that was all Donovan was trying to give me and, in return, he didn't expect anything. All this time, I had been running from Donovan, yet looking for exactly what he had been trying to give me.

I had to laugh at my own revelation. I wanted the family, the white picket fence, all the things my husband wanted to give me and more. The man wasn't my enemy; he just loved me enough to want me to have his baby.

I understood that now.

Sean's voice broke my train of thought. "What is it about him that you can't let go, Teri?"

"Seven years."

I disconnected the call and turned off my phone. I had checked in the hotel under a fake name, so even if he called every hotel downtown, he wouldn't find me.

Chapter Twenty-one

The next morning, I dialed Donovan's office.

He answered on the first ring. He sounded tired and worn. Our "War of the Roses" had gotten to both of us. It had wounded us on a level we would probably never understand. I don't think either of us expected things to spiral out of control the way they had. Now, our problems were barreling toward us like a runaway train with no conductor.

"Take me off speaker phone, please."

He picked up the phone. "Teri?"

"Yes."

"Where are you?"

"Downtown at the Georgian Terrace."

"You're right up the street from me?"

"Yes."

"How long have you been there?"

"Since I left the hospital."

"Can I please see you?"

"Room ten-oh-one."

I cleaned up the room. I packed my clothes up and shoved the suitcase in the closet. I tried to rehearse what I would say to Donovan, and how I would tell him about the pregnancy—if I was going to tell him at all.

I dumped my purse out and fished out the number to the abortion clinic Dr. Lunsford had given me. I ran my finger across the raised phone number on the off-white card. I thought about how Donovan never had to know about this pregnancy and we could start over—fresh.

The tears came in waves, pounding against my ears and causing my breath to catch in my throat.

I dialed Renee, told her what I was thinking, and asked her for help in my decision. She tried her best to console me and let me know it would be okay. She told me that the decision was mine and I had to be the one to make it.

"I don't think I can go on like this, Renee—not without Donovan."

"Then go home."

"I don't think I can."

"Teri, how do you know that that baby you're carrying isn't Donovan's?" she asked.

"Excuse me?"

"You could have very well gotten pregnant by your husband, Teri."

"I doubt it. We haven't had sex in—"

She finished what I couldn't. "Almost two months."

My body got tense. My mind hit rewind so fast I got dizzy. It took me back to the night in the hallway with my husband, our last time together.

"Renee, I don't think so."

"Come on, Teri. Don't do this. Don't go all teenager on me. Think!" she insisted.

"I'm trying!" I paced the floor as I did some bootleg math in my head. My figures weren't coming out right. I wasn't surprised as math was never my strongest subject in college.

"Teri, you could be about to abort your husband's child. Think about it."

"That just couldn't be."

"Are you ready to chance that?"

"I don't have a choice! If Sean finds out I am pregnant, he is going to insist it's his."

"I still can't believe you had sex with that man without using a condom."

"Get over it. Renee, what's done is done."

"Don't get mad at me because your life is falling apart. This is out of control."

There was a knock on the door.

"Renee, I gotta go."

"Who is that?"

I opened the door and looked into my husband's eyes. Intense feelings came flooding back, threatening to knock me down.

"My husband."

I disconnected the call as I fell into my husband's arms and cried like a baby. I cried for everything.

"It's okay, Teri," he said, smoothing my hair back. "I'm glad you called me."

"I am so sorry, Donovan."

He hugged me. He smelled incredible. He pulled his handkerchief out of his suit pocket and handed it to me.

"I guess we both messed up," he said.

"Yes . . . we have. Can it be fixed?"

"Only if you want it to be."

"I do. I do."

"Is it over between you and him?"

"Yes. I swear."

"Does this mean you are coming home?"

I nodded into his shoulder. I felt too ashamed to look at him, but he made me. His eyes were intense; love filled them as he told me he loved me and swore to work on our marriage.

"Seven years, Teri."

"I know."

As he hugged me, I caught a glimpse of myself in the mirror and hated what I saw. The baby growing inside of me would always be a constant reminder of what had happened to us.

I couldn't live like that. I wouldn't live like that.

Chapter Twenty-two

As I sat in Renee's kitchen, the wonderful smell of something good cooking floated around the room.

I hadn't eaten since the night before and I was starving. Renee was standing over the stove, wooden spoon in one hand, phone propped under her ear, and a pot top in the other. I giggled when I saw her. She turned around, told whoever she was trying to hold a conversation with that she would call them later, and hung up the phone.

"What's so funny?" she asked, stirring something that smelled incredible. I walked over and tried to peek into the pot. She tapped my hand like I was a little kid and told me to get out of her way.

"You," I said, sitting at her kitchen table. "Little Miss Suzie Homemaker."

She struck a pose like she was waiting for someone to take her picture for the front of *Family Circle* or one of those home magazines, with a huge grin on her face.

"Yup, and proud of it!" she said, turning her attention back to the bubbling stuff on the stove.

"What are you cooking?"

"Spaghetti."

Clouds of steam swirled around Renee's head. I watched her as she did her mother/wife thing. She was so happy, so content. Her apron was tied tight around her waist, and I could've sworn I heard her humming. I looked around her kitchen. Yellows, blues, and white blended together, giving the room a homey feel.

She had black and white pictures of different family scenes hanging on the wall above the table: kids playing, a father throwing a baseball to his son, a daughter in a tutu and ballet shoes. Her white on white kitchen made it seem brighter than what the small window over the sink made it. Renee didn't have a deck outside her kitchen doors like me. She had a back door that led to the backyard. Just like when we were little. All the new houses now took away from that down home feel; they were all modern and sterile.

I tapped my nails on her wooden table with the white top, reached for a napkin from the holder, and started shredding it.

"Don't make a mess, Teri," she said, never turning around.

She had eyes in the back of her head. I guess you had to with a three-year-old running around. I folded up the napkin and tossed it in her trash can.

I walked to the counter near the stove and leaned against it. I grabbed a piece of garlic bread before she could smack my hand.

"What?" she asked, with that tone that your mother used when she knew you wanted something, but were too scared to ask.

"Nothing."

"I know you, Teri. You're hovering around. What?"

I told her that my appointment was in two days and I wanted her to go with me. She closed her eyes, said a silent prayer to herself. The kind where your lips move, but nothing comes out.

"And you are sure that's best?" she asked, shaking a bottle of something into the sauce.

I munched on my bread. "I don't know, Renee. If I tell Donovan, he will be devastated. Then, what if after nine long months, it turns out to be Sean's?" I made my way to the table and sat down.

She shook her head. "You know how I feel about abortion, Teri. It's just not right."

I agreed with her. I didn't like the idea any more than she did, but I didn't have any other options. My marriage and my life were at stake now.

"What did Donovan have to say?" she asked, wiping her hands on her apron and taking a seat across from me at the table.

I sat back in my chair, and looked around at her happiness. It made me realize my life was so screwed up. "Nothing. He was just happy I had finally come home. I had to have Sean's car towed back to his house."

She rolled her eyes and made an agitated sound. "You shouldn't have had it in the first place. I can't believe you. When you decide to screw up, you do it big. I'm here for you though."

I managed a smile. "Thank you. I really needed to hear that."

She got up and made her way to check on dinner.

I pulled out my cell to check my messages. Sean had sent me two text messages asking me to call him. He even left the number to the hospital and his emergency room pager number. I deleted both of them.

Later at home, I walked around my house and smiled at how clean Donovan had kept it. He had even dusted, and I knew he hated to do that.

Sean called me three times after I left Renee's. Each time, I let him go to voicemail. Each one of his messages was more intense, more urgent. Around five, Donovan came home. He told me he wanted to take me out to dinner. I was surprised to see him home before the sun went down.

We walked into Sambuca's; he had already made reservations. I smiled at the petite hostess as she scratched our name off of her list. She led us to a table that was nestled in the back—not far from where I had sat with Sean.

"Can I get you something to drink?" she asked.

"A bottle of Zinfandel will be fine," my husband said.

I scanned the room and prayed no faces here were familiar to me; prayed I wasn't familiar to anyone else. The many smells in the restaurant mixed together, making me nauseated, I burped a little, but washed it back down with my water.

Donovan asked, "Are you okay?"

"Yes, I'm fine. This place is nice."

"A client told me about it a while ago. I have wanted to bring you here for a long time."

I smiled. "How did you end up getting off work so early?"

"Told them I had to come home and take care of my wife." He winked.

It took a little bit, but eventually we both relaxed and talked for hours. He apologized a thousand times for his part in all of this and told me that if he could take it back, he would. He assured me it was over between him and Tracie and had been for a while.

"Do you think things will ever be the same again?" I asked.

"I am going to do everything in my power to make that happen. I love you too much not to."

I bit my lip and thought about the baby inside of me. I thought about my appointment. Renee told me she would go with me, but I wasn't sure I wanted that. I felt I needed to do it by myself. I had gotten myself into this and I was going to get myself out.

"When do you plan on going back to work?" he asked as he munched on his steak.

"I don't know. I thought about staying home for a while and finding out who I am . . . A lot has happened."

"I just want you to be happy, Teri, that's all. I am not expecting you to stay home—barefoot and pregnant."

I nodded. "I know."

He told me he supported me in whatever I decided to do. Unconsciously, my hand went to my belly. I looked at my husband and imagined a little boy with his eyes, his curly hair, my smile. That image morphed. It changed to a child with the eyes of a liar and the smile of his father, the cardiologist. I shook my head, trying to erase that image.

"I was scared to death when Renee called me to let me know you were in the hospital."

I looked down as I pushed my food around on my plate.

"I am so sorry you had to go through that alone," he said.

"Renee was there."

"I know, but I wasn't."

"I just wish I knew who did it. Why they did it."

"That was a wakeup call for me. I thought I had lost you."

I managed a smile. "It's not that easy to get rid of me."

He winked. "I see."

"I am here now."

"And I thank God for that."

He pushed away from the table and told me he was going to the restroom. I was sipping on my ice water when I felt my phone vibrating in my purse. I flipped it open.

It was him.

"Yes, Sean."

"What are you doing, Teri?"

"Excuse me?"

"We need to talk."

"I am done talking to you, Sean. It's over. I am trying to get my life back."

165

"You think you are just going to turn my world upside down like you have and then walk away?"

I let out a sigh. "Sean, I am sorry. I should've never brought you into this mess."

"You have got to be kidding me."

"No, I'm not. I am trying to make things right."

"I can't let you do that, Teri."

"What do you mean, you can't *let* me?"

"I need to talk to you face to face. You're making a mistake."

"What are you talking about, Sean?"

"Call me later. Here comes your husband."

The line went dead as my husband sank into his seat. My heart was beating so fast that I could hear it in my ears. I drank my water, then took a deep breath and blinked a hundred times trying to digest what he had just said.

He was here.

Donovan asked, "Who was that?"

"Renee."

I looked around the dining room, looked back toward the kitchen, then toward the bar. That's when I saw him. His eyes locked on mine and I got dizzy. He winked at me before disappearing into the dinner crowd.

"Are you okay, Teri?"

I nodded. "I am just tired. You ready?"

"Yeah."

Chapter Twenty-three

The waiting room at the clinic was cold and sterile.

I looked around and noticed a small girl sitting in the corner below the PLEASE REFRAIN FROM CELL PHONE USE! sign. She was hunched over, on her cell. I could tell from her demeanor that she was upset with whomever she was talking to.

I sat with the clipboard full of papers on my lap, flipped them back and forth, and tried to fill in my information the best I could. By the third form, I was tired of writing my name and address and wished I had let Renee come with me.

Another girl walked in. She looked like she had been crying. She took a seat across the waiting room from me and began to try to conquer the thick stack of papers. Our eyes met, and we gave each other a weak smile. The nurse called her name.

"Santee Mitchell."

She stood like she was on autopilot as she headed in the direction of the short lady with the comforting smile.

What seemed like a lifetime later, it was my turn to take the walk.

"Teresa McCall."

The nurse called my name and I damn near jumped out of my skin. I gathered my things and followed her down the long corridor to a small exam room.

She told me to undress and gave me a paper gown to put on before leaving me alone with my demons.

I sat on the edge of the small table, scratched my head, and looked around the room. No picture of a nursing mother here—just stark white walls.

My cell phone rang. I pulled it out of my purse and saw Renee's name on the display.

"Yes, Renee."

"You there?"

"Yeah, they just brought me back."

"So it's not too late to change your mind then, right?"

"I am not changing my mind, Renee. I have to do this."

"No, you don't."

"Yes, I do."

"Donovan doesn't have to know."

I didn't like what she was proposing. I knew too many females who had gotten pregnant and then passed the baby off to some unsuspecting soul only for it to come out on *Maury* that it wasn't his. And I'd be damned if I ended up on *Maury*.

"Right, then I have a baby that has no Latino traits. How do I explain that?"

"Tell him your family has strong genes."

"Bye, Renee."

"Call me if you need me."

I bit my lip, trying to fight back the tears. I could barely understand what I was saying through the sobs when I told her I did need her. I begged my friend to come be with me.

Renee followed me home in her car. She gave me a couple of Tylenol for my headache. After fixing me some tea, she sat on the edge of the bed.

"It's okay. You are going to be fine. Do you know what you are going to tell Donovan?"

"I don't know."

"Don't get me wrong; I am happy that you decided to have the baby, but there are some real issues you need to address with your husband and with Sean."

"I know, Renee. I'll come up with something."

My friend rescued me from that clinic. Renee rolled up in there like she was FBI and seized me from the room. I told her on the phone that I couldn't do it, that I loved this baby already and I didn't want to lose it too. Without asking why, my friend was there to help me pick up the pieces of my life yet again.

"Look, I have class in an hour. I will come back after it's over. What time does Donovan get home?"

"Six."

"I will be back before then."

I dozed off, praying that when I woke up, all of this would be a dream.

My cell phone woke me around noon. I didn't even open my eyes to answer it.

"Hello."

"Teri?"

"What do you want, Sean?"

"Why won't you meet me so we can talk, Teri?"

"About what?"

"Us."

"There is no us, Sean. It's over."

"Don't say that."

"Please stop calling me, Sean. And stop following me."

"I had to see you. You have no idea how much that hurt me to see you sitting there with him, laughing and talking."

"He's my husband!"

"Bullshit! What's going to happen when you are tired of him again, or pissed off at him again? What then? I guess then it will be my turn again."

"Fuck you, Sean!"

"We already did that—remember?"

I hung up, turned my phone off, and shoved it in my nightstand drawer. He was crazier than a six dollar bill, and he obviously wasn't ready to give up.

The house phone rang and I snatched it up and answered it.

"Hello!"

"What's up? You okay?"

Donovan's voice calmed me. I swallowed my anger.

"I am fine. Just napping. Not feeling very well."

"You need me to come home?"

"No. It's probably just my period coming. I'm okay."

"Let me know if you need anything."

"Okay."

Donovan and I tried our best to reclaim our marriage. He was making it home at a decent hour, and the fact that I was still out on leave was definitely making him happy. He barely let me out of his sight to even go to the store. I had to admit that I was actually starting to like all the attention he was giving me, attention I had fought so hard to avoid before. I tried to pull strength from deep inside to tell him about the baby, but I knew that would open up a door that I had fought so hard to close. Renee told me she thought I should just tell him and leave it at that. Deal with the rest when it came up.

After about a week and a half, I was more than ready to go back to work. I needed to go back. I was tired of sitting around the house doing nothing. I had to change my cell number because Sean wouldn't stop calling me. Donovan believed that Sean and I had only slept together once, and I wanted it to stay that way. He didn't need to know that the brotha was stalking me. I called Donovan before my first appointment for the day.

"What time do you think you will be home?" he asked.

"I will be home when you get there."

"Good, I'll see you then."

"Okay."

"I love you, Teri."

"I love you too, Donovan."

That made me feel good. That was the first time in a long time I had heard those words from him and actually believed it.

After my first appointment, I dialed Renee.

"What are you doing?" I asked.

"Working on some month-end reports. What's up?"

"I don't know."

"You second guessing yourself?"

"Of course."

"It's too late now, Teri. You have to do what you have to do."

I rolled my eyes at the insinuation of me having a change of heart. I wanted this baby, but I was scared I wasn't going to get the "happily ever after" that came along with it.

"I know."

"Well, now that Sean doesn't have your number anymore, maybe his crazy behind will take the hint."

"I hope so."

"How are things at home?"

"They are okay, but that wound is still there."

"It's going to take time to heal, Teri. It's only been a couple of weeks."

"I know."

"Have you been praying?"

"I try, but I don't think God is listening."

"Don't say that, Teri. God is always listening and answering. Sometimes we just don't want to hear what he has to say."

"True."

"Once you tell Donovan you're pregnant, things will be much better."

I knew better than that and so did she. Babies don't make things better; they change things, yes, but making them better not so much.

I smiled at the thought of my trusting husband. He wanted to be a father so badly. Not knowing his father really impacted him growing up. It made him want to give back to his own child everything he didn't get from his father. His mother was great, but she couldn't give him the balance he needed.

My second line rang. I thought about not answering it.

"Renee, I gotta go."

"Hold your head up, girl. You'll be fine. It will get better."

I disconnected Renee and answered. "Dr. McCall."

"Why did you change your number?"

Sean's voice caused tension to spread through my back and settle in my shoulders. The fact that he had gone from stable doctor to psychotic stalker was blowing my mind. Talk about not being able to judge a book by its cover. And I was a psychologist! What the heck did that say about my ability?

"What do you want, Sean?"

"I need to see you."

"I can't do that."

"Yes, you can! Just give me five minutes."

"No. Good-bye, Sean!"

"Teri, just five minutes."

"Good-bye, Sean!"

I disconnected him, and then told Eva to hold all my calls. After my last session, I had the security guard walk me to my car. I was heavy and I couldn't wait to get home and wash off all the negativity.

The security guard kept apologizing about my attack, like it was his fault. I assured him that it wasn't and that I was fine.

"Well, I sho' am happy to see you back."

I handed him a tip. "I am glad to be back."

By the time I got home that evening, I was emotionally and physically drained. My head had been pounding ever since Sean called me at the office. It seemed like it was going to take a natural disaster for him to leave me alone. His whole persona had changed. He went from Prince Charming to psychopath right before my eyes. I fought hard not to blame myself.

I had danced to the music—now I had to pay the piper.

Chapter Twenty-four

The screech and wail of the alarm system brought me out of a deep sleep.

I reached for Donovan, but he wasn't there. I jumped up and ran toward the door, but before I could go any further, Donovan came in panting like he had just run a marathon.

"Are you okay?" he asked, trying to catch his breath.

"Yes, I'm fine."

I turned the light on from the switch on the wall, causing the big light in the middle of the ceiling to light up the room. I made my way back to the bed and sat down.

"What's going on?"

"Somebody broke in through the patio doors. I chased them out."

I gripped my chest. "Who was it, Donovan?"

He paced the floor. "I don't know, I didn't get a good look at them. It was too dark."

His pacing was making me dizzy. I stopped trying to follow him and walked to the window. I looked out at the perfectly manicured bushes, squinted at the shadows, and imagined I saw a thousand different figures. I got scared. I wondered if Sean was capable of breaking into my house.

I looked back at Donovan. He was sitting on the edge of the bed, leg bouncing with fists balled. He was a king whose castle had just been invaded.

I turned my attention back to the street outside of my window. I watched cars come and go and listened to the hum of the highway. I couldn't help but wonder if the person was still out there. The phone rang and made me jump. Donovan answered it, and I heard him giving our alarm code to the person on the other side. He assured them that we were fine before hanging up.

"Teri, come away from the window," he said, walking over and closing the blinds.

In the blink of an eye, Cobb County's finest had descended on my home. Chaos sliced into the night air with no respect for the time. I sat on the couch in a trance. My eyes kept cutting to the front door that was wide open. Every time I looked, a different cop was in the doorway. Night air flooded my home, turning it into a house. I felt like I was in the middle of a horror movie. I heard an officer's radio squawk as they moved through my space. I sat staring as Donovan talked to one of the cops. I could see lips moving, but couldn't hear or understand what they were saying.

A female officer came and sat next to me. She asked me a few questions. I answered the best I could, but my head was throbbing and my mouth was dry.

At one point, I looked up and noticed Renee moving through the confusion. She was carrying a bottle of water and talking on her cell, probably to her mother.

She asked, "Are you okay?"

All I could do was nod.

I heard her voice, but couldn't make out what she was saying. I felt like I was packed in cotton. I took a sip of the water she handed me.

After the police left, my friend was in the kitchen cleaning. I tried to stop her, but I didn't have the strength. Donovan was on the phone with the alarm company. He cupped the phone and told me to go lay down. I didn't want to, but my body had other plans, and I went to the couch. I lay down and listened to the bustle in my house while I drifted off to sleep.

The next day, I was antsy. I kept checking and re-checking doors and locks. Donovan said he wasn't going to be home until six and it was barely three. I tried to occupy my time reading and surfing the web, but I couldn't seem to sit still. I called Renee, but she was in a meeting.

"Let me call you when I get finished," she whispered into the phone.

"Okay. Just hurry up."

I hung up, stood in front of my mirror, shoved a pillow under my shirt, and pretended it was full of life. A wave washed over me, choking me, and pushing tears up and out. I was supposed to be happy, not regretful.

The phone rang, pulling me from my pity party. I looked at the caller ID. It read: CRAWFORD LONG HOSPITAL. He must've gotten my home number from the hospital records.

I snatched up the phone. "What do you want, Sean?"

"I already told you."

"What do you want to talk about?"

"No, we do this in person."

I looked at my watch. Donovan wasn't going to be home for at least another three hours. He had a conference call that involved the West Coast. Something about time difference, client's availability, yadda yadda yadda. In a nutshell, I was going to have to be at home by myself longer than I wanted to. So I agreed, for no other reason than to get out of the house.

"Where, Sean?"

"Dugan's on Ponce in an hour."

"One hour. I am waiting no more than two minutes, then I am out."

"Fair enough."

I headed up Piedmont and made a right onto Ponce. There were all kinds of people walking up and down Ponce, mostly streetwalkers and hustlers.

I passed Zesto's and thought about all the times I had been there for an ice cream cone. It amazed me how easily eating an ice cream cone could transform you into a little kid. It always took me back to the days of playing kick ball in front my grandmother's house, and sounds of Run DMC echoing from a nearby car. It was a feeling I would give anything to have right now. I wanted to be that little girl again, without a care in the world.

The parking lot at Dugan's was packed. I was hoping I could catch Sean outside so I didn't have to go in. He was sitting in his CLK when I pulled up, and he looked like he was reading something.

I pulled into the parking space across from him, causing him to look up. I left my car running. I didn't want to stay long, and I wanted him to know that. I wanted to squash whatever was driving him toward insanity and get back home.

He got out and walked to my driver's side window. I hit the automatic window button and let it down. He leaned over and rested his arms on the door. His Burberry cologne invaded my nose and the inside of my car.

"Are you going to get out?" he asked.

"No, I can't. I am supposed to be meeting Renee. What do you want?"

He stepped back, admired my car. He looked from me to it, then back again.

"I see you got your car back."

I sucked my teeth. "Whatever. What do you want?"

"Let's go get some wings. Give me thirty minutes."

"No, Sean."

His demeanor changed. Hardened. His eyes filled with anger. His tone was demanding. "Get out of the car, Teri."

I looked up at him. I saw something in his eyes

that scared me to death, but I didn't want to back down. "Excuse you?"

I revved my engine, letting him know that he was about to get run over.

"Would you just get out of the car and come talk to me? I just want to clear things up between us."

Against my better judgment, I turned the engine off and checked my watch. I didn't want this to run any longer than it needed to.

He said, "Don't worry, you will be home before his punk ass."

I pushed my door open, purposely hitting him with it. He just laughed it off and walked toward the steps leading to the entrance.

I followed him, but not before I made sure I had my cell phone and felt around for the pepper spray in my purse. Hopefully, this would be it. I prayed that once he said what he had to say, he would leave me alone.

We found a booth in the back. The waitress smiled, acknowledging us as she took another couple's order. She really didn't need to come to our table because I didn't plan on being there long enough to order anything.

"What do you want, Sean?" I asked as I slid into the seat.

He sat across from me, looking at me or through me. It was hard to know which one.

"I want you to think about what you are doing. Why are you going back to him?"

"Sean, we have had this conversation so many times before. Come on now. It's getting old."

"I love you, Teri."

I shook my head, letting him know I wasn't buying it. "No, you don't."

He looked around the dining room, shifted around in his seat, reached up, and scratched his head. "There is something I need to know."

I sighed. "What?"

He leaned forward and gave me anominous smile. "Okay. How about this? How would your husband feel knowing that you are pregnant by another man?"

My throat got tight and it became hard to breathe. I tried to speak but couldn't. He just sat there nodding, telling me how he pulled my chart and saw the pregnancy results.

I grabbed my purse and started to slide out of the booth. He reached across and grabbed my arm.

"Where are you going?"

"Home to my *husband*!" I snapped. "Let me go."

"What do you plan on telling old hubby when you push out another man's seed?"

Anger and hurt flashed across his face like a bad movie. I wanted to get as far away from him as I could. I wished I could do an *I Dream of Jeannie* and blink him to some island off the coast of Zimbabwe. I pulled my arm, but he just tightened his grip.

Fire consumed me. I became a lioness whose cub was being threatened. There was no way this psychopath was getting his hands on me or my baby.

Something inside of me snapped.

"I won't have to tell him anything, because there's not going to be a baby. I got rid of it!" I said through clenched teeth. "Now let me go!"

I snatched my arm so hard it slammed into my chest. He sat there, mouth open. He was speechless. I leaned into him and told him to stay away from me— and to lose my phone number. I threatened to call the police, the hospital, Oprah, whomever I had to call to get him to leave me alone.

"You had an abortion, Teri?" His tone was soft; hurt filled his eyes. His demeanor softened. What we had done was killing both of us. It was no longer about me or my happiness; it was about the secret I carried deep inside.

"Yes, I did." I responded, completing my circle of lies. "You have to leave me alone. It's over. What we had is over."

I turned and walked away, fueled partly by fear, but mostly by a desire to be home with my husband. I had to tell him about the baby I was carrying—his baby. It just had to be.

Sean called to my back as I walked away, "It's not over, Teri, believe that!"

I sped away from Dugan's feeling like the weight of the world had been lifted off my shoulders.

I had no idea how wrong I was.

Chapter Twenty-five

"Do you think he will back off?" Renee asked.

"I hope so."

We sat at my kitchen table, sharing a spread of Chinese food that we had just ordered, trying to recapture some of the peace of mind that had been lost.

"He's a damn nut."

I nodded. "He needs to focus on some other chick and leave me alone."

"What did he say when you told him you had an abortion?"

"Told me it wasn't over."

Her eyes got wide. "What did you say?"

"Nothing. I let him sit at the table looking like a fool."

She got up and grabbed a Corona off the counter.

"You better be careful with him. I don't want to have to knock him out."

"Thanks, Tyson."

Donovan called to check on me. I told him that Renee was at the house and was actually surprised he wasn't mad. He promised he would be home as soon as his meeting was over. I told him to hurry because I needed to talk to him.

I got excited at the thought of his reaction—us hugging, making love. Him fussing over me, rubbing my feet, talking about the soon-to-be and the whats to come.

Renee asked, "Are you going to tell Donovan about Sean?"

"Girl! No!"

"I think you should. What if something happens. He needs to know."

I shook my head. "I can't do that."

"Well, if something happens to you, how do you think that is going to affect him?"

There was no way I could tell him that it was more than once. That would kill him. I know it would. We had dealt with so much hurt and pain. I was ready for all of it to just go away.

Too many thoughts came to me at once, I couldn't seem to focus, so I got up and reached for a bottle of Corona. Renee's voice shrieked. She made a sound like the world was ending, and I almost dropped the glass bottle on the floor.

"What is wrong with you?" I asked, looking at her like she was crazy.

"You can't drink that." She took the bottle from my hand and replaced it with a bottle of Dasani. "There you go, pregnant lady."

I smiled. "Wow, I forgot."

"I can't wait to see you all fat and cranky."

"That was you."

"Whatever. Christopher did a number on me. I had hemorrhoids and I was constipated. I couldn't even sleep at night, thanks to his big behind."

I laughed at that memory. Renee had gained so much weight, she had developed gestational diabetes and her doctor cut her menu down to nothing. I remember her sneaking cheesecake and timing it just right so it wouldn't show up on her diabetes test at her next doctor's visit.

"I refuse to get as big as you were." I laughed.

"Whatever. You get whatever that baby decides to put on you. You know, if it's a girl they steal your beauty; if it's a boy, they make you gain weight to help bulk them up."

"So I am either going to be an ugly pregnant lady or a big fat one? Is that what you're saying?"

She laughed. "Just stating the facts."

"You're so crazy."

"When are you going to tell Donovan?"

"I am thinking about tonight."

"What do you think he will say?"

"I don't know. I hope he is so happy that he will want to move to Cuba; then I won't have to deal with Sean."

"You can't run from him. He is going to have to be dealt with, Teri."

"Yeah, yeah. I know."

Donovan got home around nine-thirty. I had talked myself into and out of telling him about the pregnancy a hundred times. Renee told me to let him know tonight and to call her in the morning. She said something about bagging up all of Christopher's baby stuff. I was so not ready for that right now, so I just tuned her out.

When Donovan came in, I was lying on the bed, trying to digest the Chinese food I had just eaten. My stomach was bubbling more than a hot tub at the Playboy mansion. I guess he could tell I didn't feel well.

"Are you okay?"

"We ate Chinese; now my stomach is upset."

He laughed. "I told you about eating that stuff. That's why I don't mess with it. You need anything?"

I surveyed my husband and saw how happy he was, how content he was with where we were going with our relationship. The fact that we were working on it was all he ever wanted, and that was evident to me now.

I touched his hand and asked him to sit down so I could talk to him.

"What's up?" he said, removing his suit jacket.

"I don't quite know how to say this, so I am going to just spit it out."

I took a deep breath; my mind started racing. So many thoughts, so many emotions, I felt like I was about to short circuit. I thought about what Renee said. I was going to have to be prepared to stand by whatever I said, not wavering, and making sure that Sean was a distant memory. I didn't know how Donovan would handle the truth.

His attention was on me, making me anxious.

So anxious, that I vomited right there, in my husband's lap.

Chapter Twenty-six

"You're what?"

After I cleaned up and my husband showered, I managed to composed myself and tell him what I was trying to say when my food decided to show up for an encore performance. The look he gave me was hard to translate. I didn't get the ecstatic fanfare that I had imagined, but he didn't toss me out on my pregnant behind either.

He stood up, walked toward the lounge chair, and rested his weight on it for a second before looking at me.

"I . . . uh . . . I'm pregnant." I said, fidgeting with the tag on the comforter. Tears welled in my eyes, as fear told me that my husband wasn't happy and convinced me that I should have gone with my first instinct and had the abortion.

Sometime during my internal beat down, my husband came to me and hugged me. He told me that he was happy and we were going to be okay.

"How far along are you?" he asked.

"Almost twelve weeks."

"Wow. I'm going to be a father?" His tone was questioning, like he still didn't believe what he had heard. Like he was looking for confirmation.

I nodded.

He said it again. "Wow."

I got up, as nervous energy moved me across the room to gather the sheets I messed up with my vomiting routine. He jumped up and took them from me.

"I can wash them," he said.

I smiled. "Donovan, you don't have to do that. I am capable of turning on the machine without hurting myself."

"I know, it's just . . . "

I touched his face, found the fear that lived in his eyes from losing our daughter, understood it, and tried to comfort it. I promised him I wouldn't overdo it, and that I was going to turn down the offer for partner at the practice and cut back my patients until after the baby was born. That seamed to ease his mind and brought a smile to his face, but he still took the soiled sheets and washed them himself.

I took that opportunity to call Renee and tell her what happened. I could hear her smiling through the phone. She was still emotional about Derrick leaving, and she cried when she told me how happy she was.

"Teri, I told you things would work out."

"Yes, you did. I am just happy that he took it well."

"I bet you are. Have you heard from Sean?"

"He left me a message this afternoon."

"Okay, just be careful, please."

"I will."

"You know we have to go shopping, right, and we have to start planning your nursery, and—"

"Whoa! Slow down, Renee. Let a sister start taking prenatal vitamins first. One step at a time."

"You're not taking your vitamins?"

"No, they make me nauseous. The smell alone makes me want to throw up."

"Try taking them at night with orange juice. That helped me."

We chatted for a little while about whether I thought it was a boy or girl, which room I would paint

186

for the nursery, and names. She liked Imani for a girl; I hated it. I told her I liked the name Anna.

"Ewww, what kind of name is Anna?"

"Heifer, that was my grandmother's name."

"Oh." She laughed. "My bad."

"Look, I am going to go to sleep. I will call you back in the morning."

"Do that. Maybe we can meet for lunch."

"As long as it ain't Chinese."

"Deal."

I went to check on Donovan. He had fallen asleep in his recliner. I told him I was going to bed, and he promised he would be up in a few. I checked the locks on the doors in the kitchen, made sure the windows were secure before making my way back toward the steps.

I managed to slip into work the next day barely noticed. I was dreading talking to Dr. Lee because I wasn't sure how he was going to take what I had to say. So I decided to send him an e-mail.

Boy, you gotta love Bill Gates. He made it really easy to hide behind e-mails.

"Are you nervous?" Renee asked.

"Just a little."

I called her after I hit send and told her about the promise I made to my husband. She thought it was a good idea.

"Hell, he basically rescinded his offer anyway after he got those pictures, right?"

"True."

"So the hell with him and his morals." She laughed.

"I know, but I like my job. I am going to hate it if I lose it."

Eva buzzed me and told me that Monica was holding on line one. I told Eva to go ahead and schedule her an appointment and I would call her later.

Renee asked. "When is your next appointment?"

"Next week," I said, digging around in my purse for some gum. "Look, let me go. I got a one o'clock coming in."

"The clown freak?"

I couldn't help but laugh. "Don't say that, Renee. He's a nice man."

"Come on, Teri. *Clowns*?"

I laughed. "I'll call you later."

I sat at my desk and played the scenario over and over again in my mind. I thought about how it would be to quit, then imagined myself waddling around the office, munching on fries and keeping my job. Realistically, I couldn't see past right now, and my memory wouldn't let me erase the image of Sean Morris.

The phone on my desk rang, making me jump. I picked it up, expecting to hear Renee's voice.

"Hello."

"Teri, don't hang up."

With the sound of Sean's voice, my body tensed. I felt warm. I stood up, uncomfortable in my office. I looked toward the door and noticed a few people in the hall. Having them around made me feel a little better. I wondered if he was the one who broke into my house that night.

"Leave me alone, Sean, please!"

"I want to talk to you. Can I see you?"

"No, Sean, are you crazy? I told you to stop calling me."

"I can't do that, Teri. I need to see you."

"Why?"

"I just want to know what went wrong. How could you abort my child?"

That made me queasy. I had tried so hard to convince myself that this baby wasn't his, and re-opening that wound would set me back weeks in my brainwashing.

I gathered my things up and tried to end the call so I could get home to my husband.

"Look, I don't think we have anything to talk about. What's done is done."

"Teri, please. Just give me five minutes of your time."

"No, Sean."

His tone changed. "Either you talk to me, or I talk to your husband. What's it going to be?"

I wanted to scream, shout, and throw a tantrum, anything to get through to him. I didn't need him seeking out Donovan, which would make things worse than they already were.

"Leave him out of this."

"You know what to do then."

I thought about my husband and felt sorry for him, for the things I had done. I hated that both of us had put our marriage in jeopardy the way we had. Depression was looming, I could tell. She had darkened my doorstep before, and I had found the only way to get rid of her was to confront her head on.

"Don't do this."

"Ever since you told me about . . . " His words stuck in his throat. "I can't stop thinking about you."

"I told you, we wouldn't work. I am still married. We are trying to work on our marriage. I can't just walk away from seven years, Sean."

"I love you, Teri."

Every time I convinced myself that it was over and that I would be able to handle having the baby with my husband, whether it was Donovan's or not, Sean popped up. He was a constant reminder, like the herpes virus. Just when you think it's gone—BAM—you have a flare up.

My plan was to have the baby, with the hope that over the next six months Sean would get it and leave me be. I wanted him to forget about me, and then I could really get on with my life. He wasn't cooperating at all.

"I'm hanging up, Sean. Please stop harassing me." I picked my cell up off my desk and looked at the clock. It was almost five-thirty. I needed to get home. As if he knew I was thinking about him, my phone vibrated in my hand. HOME flashed on the screen.

"Oh, that's what I am doing now?"

"Look, I just want to get on with my life with my husband."

I felt nothing but regret for what happened. The life in my uterus was a product of the mess I had made and I had to deal with the fallout.

"Teri, I can't let you go."

"You have to, Sean. This is crazy. Good-bye."

I hung up and headed home. All the way driving home, I kept telling myself that everything would be okay.

But deep down, I knew that wasn't true.

Chapter Twenty-seven

The next day, I sat in my office, head in hands, wanting to scream.

I was waiting for Monica. She was my only appointment for the day and I was glad. I was tired and couldn't keep food down to save my life. Donovan tried to talk me into staying home, but I promised him that after her appointment, I was coming right back home.

A tap on my door made me look up. Monica was standing in the door smiling.

"Hello, Monica. Come on in."

I ran my fingers through my hair and tucked it behind my ears. I tried to get myself together, hoping we would have a productive session and I could make a clean getaway. Dr. Lee had been trying to pin me down ever since I told him I was going to pass on becoming a partner. I wasn't ready to face him yet, so I had been screening all e-mails and calls.

"What's wrong?" she asked. "You don't look good."

"You're right. I don't." I stood up. "Would you mind if we rescheduled?"

I almost hated to reschedule with her. We had been making really good progress. She was doing well, and I was pretty sure her self-esteem was improving. I almost felt like I was letting her down by rescheduling, but then I'd let a lot of people down, so I guess she shouldn't be any different.

She stood up and tucked her purse under her arm. She gave me a warm smile. "No problem. I will call to reschedule."

I was powering down my PC when my phone rang. I damn near jumped and latched onto the ceiling. I hit the blinking button and tried to sound as professional as I could while wanting to vomit all over my desk. "Dr. McCall."

"Hello, doctor. Congratulations on your pregnancy."

I asked, "Who is this?" The distorted voice on the other end sounded more like something you would hear at a carnival than on the other end of a phone conversation.

"Did you get your back door fixed?"

Before I could say anything, the line went dead.

I sped through downtown and tried to track down Renee. I finally caught up with her. She was at her mother's house, picking up Christopher. I told her about my phone call and tried to control my fear as she attempted to help me figure out who it was.

"Who else knows about your pregnancy?"

"No one."

"Well, obviously somebody does. And they know about a lot more than just the baby."

"You think?" I snapped at my friend.

"Look, don't get mad at me. You still don't know who sent those pictures to Donovan, or to your boss. There is someone out there that knows about you and Sean," she said.

"I am not mad at you. I just want this to go away."

"Teri, you are going to have to own up to your part in this mess too. You and your desire for a distraction is why all this started."

I knew she was right, but it was too late to fix it. If I came clean now, I was going to lose everything. I didn't want that to happen.

That night, I called Dr. Lee and told him that

effective immediately, I was on maternity leave. I made sure to remind him of my past miscarriage and assured him that my husband and I were just taking precautions early.

Donovan was so happy that he took the next day off work to stay home with me.

We spent the next evening walking the mall and window shopping for baby furniture. He got tired of my oohs and aahs and made a break for the sporting goods store to look for some golf clubs. I found Macy's and looked for another pair of maternity pants. My stomach was growing faster than weeds in the South. With every kick and every flip of the baby inside of me, the realism of my situation came flooding back. I wanted to vomit every time I thought about Sean, and it had nothing to do with morning sickness. I found the maternity section and browsed the racks. I ended up with a purse full of makeup and a hundred-fifty dollar pair of pants.

In the food court, I told Donovan what I had bought.

"One hundred-fifty dollars, Teri?"

I batted my eyes. "I needed a treat!"

"A treat? You should've bought a damn candy bar!"

"Whatever!" I shook my head and started eating my slice of pizza. This was the first time that my husband and I had actually come to the mall for Chinese food and I didn't eat any. I couldn't eat it. I could barely stand the smell of it. The smell of teriyaki chicken and noodles wasn't the only thing bothering me. I couldn't get my mind off of Sean.

While I was eating, I looked up just as Sean walked past our table. I saw him, but Donovan didn't because his back was to Sean.

He was alone.

No bags.

Nothing that hinted that he was at the mall to shop.

The Lies that Bind

His stride was fueled by a broken heart and what could only be described as the need for revenge.

Chapter Twenty-eight

"I can't believe how big you are getting."

I laughed at my friend and rubbed my rounded belly. I had met Renee for lunch at the Cheesecake Factory. The restaurant was packed. It had been almost two months and most of the weird calls had trickled off, but Sean made his presence known as often as he could. If he wasn't calling, he was texting. Donovan hired security to watch the house, which definitely made me feel better when he worked late nights, but I still hated the reason behind all of the intrusions.

"Girl, I am starving," I said.

"I know you are."

"How are things at home?"

I scanned the menu. "Good. Better. I think the pregnancy has helped."

"Good."

"I just hate the circumstances." I sipped my water.

"I know you do. It'll work out. "

"I don't know, Renee. Sean's following me now. Donovan has security at the house and doesn't even know the full reason why. He thinks it's just a result of the break-in."

Her eyes got big. "What!"

I nodded. "I don't know what to do. I can't tell Donovan."

"Teri, you have to."

I shook my head. "If he finds out the truth—that I slept with Sean more than once—he is going to flip."

She let out a heavy sigh. "Damn, Teri. This is crazy."

I sat back in my chair. "Tell me about it."

"Well, you can't continue like this. You are pregnant now and you have that baby to think about."

I looked around the restaurant and tried to focus on the waitress stand to avoid crying. I looked at my friend through teary eyes. "I don't know what to do."

She reached over and touched my hand. "It's gonna be okay. We'll figure something out. Let's just eat right now, okay?"

Like a small child, I just nodded.

After we finished lunch, we made our way to Little Five Points. We browsed the eclectic shops that lined the streets and checked out the even more eclectic crowd of people who populated the spot. The area reminded me of the Land of Misfit Toys from the movie *Rudolph the Red-Nosed Reindeer*. It was a melting pot where anything and everything went and no one was judged. Whether your hair was pink or jet black, you were welcomed.

Renee bought a couple of antique-looking blouses and a few CDs that she found in a sale bin. I was amazed she found anything. Usually those bins held stuff like Wayne Newton's *Greatest Hits*.

I felt my phone vibrate. Sean's home number flashed across the caller ID, and I became agitated and hot. Some way he had gotten my cell phone number.

On the way back to Renee's, she said, "You think if you ignore him long enough he will go away?"

"What do you mean?"

"You know what I am talking about. That was Sean, wasn't it?"

"Yes. So?"

"So nothing, Teri. He isn't going to stop."

"I know, Renee."

"You are playing with fire. I think you would come out better if you would just tell Donovan the truth."

"What?"

"You heard me. I know you're scared of what it's going to do to your marriage, but don't you think he would rather hear the truth now, from you, instead of later, from some psycho?" she asked. "I mean, this is getting deep. You got him stalking you and someone broke into your house. Donovan needs to know."

I paused. "I understand that, Renee."

"I don't think you do."

"Fine. I'll think about it. Okay?"

She didn't say anything for a moment. "This is not going to go away on its own, Teri."

I didn't say anything.

"Teri, I am just trying to be real."

"Can we drop it, please?"

"Fine."

We rode the rest of the way to her house in silence—pissed off silence. Even while I loaded my bags from our shopping spree into my own trunk, she didn't have much to say. She hugged me, told me she loved me, and that was why she was so concerned.

I got into my car and drove away. I was thinking about Sean and wondering how things had gotten so out of control. My marriage was on the line—my baby was on the line.

He had to stop.

If I was going to take control of my life, it had to be now, because if I didn't, I was going to lose everything. The only person who could right this wrong was me, if I had any plans of having that happily ever after with my husband.

So I picked up the phone and I dialed Sean's number.

Chapter Twenty-nine

With each sound of the ringing phone, the pace of my heart rate quickened. I ran my finger along the seam of my pants, rolled it back and forth in my fingers, and hoped he wouldn't answer.

He did.

"Hello, Miss Lady."

"Sean, why are you doing this to me? Why won't you stop calling me? It's been almost two months!"

"Teri, do you have any idea how much you hurt me?"

He sounded different—desperate. I had dealt with people like him before in sessions. I knew the best thing to do was to let them vent and get it out, then try to rationalize.

"Sean, it couldn't have worked. You knew that when all this started."

My stomach was doing somersaults, and it wasn't the baby. There were so many life-changing things that were happening and it was too much for me. Something as beautiful as pregnancy had been trivialized by the ugly choices we had made. A child who didn't ask to be born was coming, no matter who its father was.

"This is not how it was supposed to happen."

"What are you talking about? How *what* was supposed to happen?"

"Just forget it. This is all wrong, Teri. Oh, and I

know about the security at your house. Tell Donovan that's a nice touch."

"Fuck you, Sean."

He laughed at me. "Do you think that a man sitting in a car can keep me from you?"

"I don't know what you want me to do, Sean. I am not going to walk away from my husband. I did that once and I will never do it again."

"Well, you and your husband should've thought about that before you both decided to screw up someone else's life."

"You leave Donovan out of this!"

"Why? It's been about him from the beginning. Right, Teresa?"

The tone of his voice made my skin crawl.

"Go to hell, Sean."

"If I go, I'm taking your husband with me."

I snapped, "What is that supposed to mean?"

"If you're not here in thirty minutes, you're going to find out." With that, he hung up.

Before I knew it, I grabbed my coat and was headed north on I-85.

I kept checking my cell phone, waiting for it to ring, but it wouldn't. My grandmother always told me that a watched pot never boils. I had left Donovan three messages and he hadn't called me back yet. Sean's voice was resonating through my mind, and I was starting to fear not only for myself, but now, for my husband.

I kept rubbing my belly, trying to calm the unrest that it held. I had no idea what I was going to say. I just hoped that he would see how much I loved my baby and my husband and agree to let me be, even if this baby turned out to be his.

I called him back and I told him that I wasn't going to come to his house, but I would meet him at Gwinnett Place Mall. There was an O'Charley's there. I figured he wouldn't nut up in a public place.

The restaurant was crowded. People were laughing and enjoying each other's company like they didn't have a care in the world.

I sidestepped a little girl who was running from her father as they made their way to the door. She was laughing so hard she could barely keep her balance. There was a look of contentment and happiness on the tall man's face as he pretended to run after her.

I noticed her mother trailing behind, her pregnant belly leading the way. Judging from the size of her womb, I could tell she didn't have much time. We smiled at each other as we passed by. I started to ask her what it felt like to be happy and free of worries, but decided against it. I didn't need her thinking I was crazy.

I noticed Sean before he saw me. He was seated at a small, two-person table near the back. His back was to me, but I could tell from his posture that he was restless and tense. I saw him reach up and scratch his head, then check his watch. I was only a few minutes late, but I knew he thought I wasn't going to show up. I nervously adjusted my coat and headed in his direction.

He stood up when he saw me.

I slid into the wooden chair across from him. The waitress smiled at me, acknowledging me as she took another table's order. I returned her smile.

"Sean, the only reason I am here is to beg you to leave us alone," I started. "I'm pregnant and I really don't need this stress."

He blinked a few times, looked at me like he didn't know who I was, and then sat back in his seat and crossed his arms. I still didn't know what to say, but I was hoping whatever I said made sense.

The waitress came and interrupted us. I ordered water with lemon; Sean ordered something a little stronger.

"Sean, I am really trying to fix my marriage. I really need for you to understand that."

"So you thought telling me you aborted my baby was going to make this go away?"

"I don't know what I thought. I guess . . . yes, I did."

"You think I am honestly going to walk away now?"

"I have to ask you to."

"What, and let you and your husband raise my baby?" He shook his head. "Not gonna happen."

"Sean, I am begging you, please, just let us get on with our lives."

"No, Teri. I can't believe you even came at me with this bullshit."

"I am trying to make this right."

"No, you are trying to make this go away, trying to act like I don't exist."

"That's not true."

"What is hubby going to say when that baby doesn't look anything like him?"

I said, "Sean, there is no guarantee that this is your baby. There is a chance that it's my husband's."

"Is that the best that you could come up with?"

"I am not trying to come up with anything. I am just being honest."

Those words hurt him. His posture straightened for a second as he let what I had just said sink in.

The waitress reappeared, saving me from whatever comeback he had for what I said. He took a long drink of the liquor he had just ordered. I sipped on my water and felt my baby kick, adding insult to injury.

"So you want me to disappear into the shadows? Is that it?"

"Just please, let me work this out my way."

"And what if it is mine, Teri? Are you going to let me know, let me be a part of its life?"

"I . . . I don't know, Sean."

"What do you mean, you don't know?"

"Just what I said; I don't know."

He stood up and tossed a twenty dollar bill on the table. He looked at me and for the first time, I felt hatred coming from him.

"You need to call and talk to your husband. I think you might find the conversation enlightening."

"What is that supposed to mean?"

He turned and disappeared into the sea of people that had begun to gather in the restaurant. I sat there for a second before heading back out into the cold to my car. I couldn't let him tell Donovan before me, but I also didn't think I had the strength to tell him myself.

On the way home, I turned on my cell phone. There were five messages. Four were hang-ups. I could hear movement, but no one said anything. The last one was from Renee, telling me she needed to talk to me. My phone vibrated in my hand. It was Renee.

"Hello."

"Where are you?"

She told me she had stopped by my house looking for me.

"I went to meet Sean."

"You did what?"

I broke down and cried as I told my friend what happened. I hoped that I hadn't made a mistake; she tried to assure me I didn't because he had a right to know the truth, no matter what.

"What if he already called Donovan? What am I going to do?"

"You are going to deal with it. You made this mess, Teri. Now it's time to own it and fix it. Whatever happens is meant to happen."

The last thing I wanted to hear was some religious psychobabble, so I told her I would call her back and I hung up.

I pulled into my driveway. Donovan was already home. I had no idea how long he had been there, but for some reason I felt better about the fact that he was.

When I got in the house, Donovan was in the kitchen. I called out to him as I pulled my poncho over my head and tossed it on the couch in the den. The

202

white-on-white furniture and lighting made the room seem like a scene in a dream.

"Hey."

I jumped and turned around at the sound of his voice. He was still in his work clothes, minus the tie. His eyes held something that I couldn't make out. He stared at me and I stared back absentmindedly. Sean's voice resonated through my mind: *I think you might find the conversation enlightening.* What did that mean?

He asked me, "Are you hungry?"

"A little."

He continued to stand there, not saying anything, just looking at me. I got hot; my face felt like I just opened the door to the oven while cooking a turkey. He turned and headed to the dining room. I followed like I was in a trance. I wasn't sure what I was walking into, but Renee was right—I had to face whatever it was.

The table was set with baked chicken and vegetables, healthy foods that a pregnant woman should be eating. The crystal sparkled and the china glowed in the dim track lighting.

My mind was digesting what Sean said about talking to my husband. I still didn't know what he meant by that. Donovan's behavior was making me more uncomfortable than a pregnant woman needed to be. I slid into one of the chairs and stared down at the food resting on the plate.

I picked up my glass and took a sip of my water.

"You should really eat, Teri. You haven't been eating right lately."

I whispered, "I know."

His next statement made my breath catch in my throat.

"I talked to Sean tonight."

I wasn't sure what to say, so I didn't say anything.

"Anything you want to tell me?" he asked.

I pushed my plate away and faced my husband.

"Donovan, I swear, it's over. I am just trying to get our life back in order."

"Is that right?"

"Yes, it is."

"He claims that he loves you. He wants to be with you." He asked, "Do you love him?"

"No, Donovan, I love you."

The look he gave me unnerved me and made me want to run from the house screaming and crying.

"I thought you said that you only slept with him once, Teri."

"I . . . I—"

I couldn't find the words. I knew what I wanted to say. I wanted my husband to understand how sorry I was, how much of a mistake I had made, but the words got caught in my throat.

"Why does he have reason to think that the baby you are carrying is his, Teri?"

"Donovan, please let me explain."

"Explain what? How you lied?"

"It's not that simple." Tears stung my eyes.

"What, you wanna explain how you fucked another man after you told me it was over?"

"Donovan—"

"Oh, I know!" He held his hands up. "You wanna try to explain how you have no idea who the father of that baby is?"

My mouth fell open but no words came out. I could barely breathe, let alone talk. His words were coming at me so fast, I couldn't make them out. My hearing was muffled, my vision was cloudy. It felt like my air was being cut short. The whole thing was made worse when my cell rang. I swallowed hard, trying to ignore it.

"You can't continue to act like he doesn't exist, Teri."

"What?"

"Answer the phone."

I slid the phone toward me and slowly picked it up off the table. I touched the screen but didn't say anything.

"You a'ight?" the all too familiar voice asked.

I wanted to scream at him, call him names that I would normally be too embarrassed to say, but my husband's glare had me frozen—frozen in a moment that wouldn't end. I swallowed, made a sound that let him know I heard him and that I got it.

"Sean, I am so sorry that all this happened."

I looked at Donovan. He was stewing like a pot when the liquid bubbles to the top and spills on to the hot stovetop, making that crackling and sizzling sound. He never took his eyes off of me.

"Teri, you have the power to make it right."

"Sean, you have to stop. You can't keep acting this way. This is over. I told you, I want to be with my husband."

"Please, you know that nigga doesn't love you, Teri! If he did, he would fight for you. He wouldn't have hung up on me like a punk when I told him about our baby."

I tried to stop the tears, but they just kept coming— in waves, it seemed. "Sean, please stop saying that."

Donovan stood to his feet and slowly made his way to my side of the table. I tensed and clutched my phone so tight that I thought the battery was going to pop off the back.

Before I could scream, he snatched the phone from me and began threatening to do things to Sean that would have him in jail for life if he didn't stay away from me.

I tried to grab the phone from him. He turned his body, blocking me with his large frame. He continued yelling into the phone. "I swear, you come near my wife again and I will kill you!"

He pitched my phone up against the wall, shattering it into pieces. All of his anger and rage turned in my direction. Tears streamed as I tried to speak through my heavy heart. He stopped my flow cold.

"Teri, don't—say—anything."

"Donovan, please let me explain."

"There is nothing to explain. I think he covered it."

"No, he didn't. He is *trying* to break us up. This is what he wants to happen."

"Why, Teri?"

"I don't know. You are asking me a question that only he knows the answer to."

"Do you love him?"

"No."

"Don't lie to me, Teri."

I leaned against the table. "I said no."

"Come on, Teri, it had to be love. You gave up the pussy and you didn't use a *condom*."

My husband's voice cracked. I could tell he was fighting back tears.

"I don't love him, Donovan. Did you love Tracie?"

He shot me a look. "Don't." His jaw clenched. "This isn't about her."

"Isn't it, Donovan? Isn't that what started this screwed up parallel universe that we seem to be stuck in?"

"Teri, you're pregnant!"

I walked to the den with him on my heels. I felt like the walls were about to cave in on me and I needed to get out.

"Don't run from this, Teri."

"I am not running from anything. This is crazy."

"Answer my question."

"There isn't one answer. One reason."

"Is it his baby, Teri?"

"No!" I let out a sigh. Rubbed my forehead. "I don't know."

"How many times, Teri?"

206

"I—" I couldn't bring myself to tell my husband the truth."

His jaw flexed and his hands opened and closed into tight fists. I sat on the couch. My back was starting to ache. I felt like a bomb had gone off inside of me. I touched my abdomen. I felt sorry for the life inside of me, sorry for the chaos that I was bringing him or her into.

"Donovan, I didn't intentionally set out to hurt you."

"And he didn't do what he did because he had nothing else to do. Do you know why he did it?"

"I don't know."

"He told me he loves you."

"Well, you asked him and he gave you an answer."

"Well, when am I going to get one from you? Do you love him?"

"I told you, no!"

"Then what was it? Lust . . . a good fuck . . . what? Why'd you go back more than once?"

"Donovan, I am not having this conversation."

"At first, I almost understood you being vindictive, trying to get back at me, but what I can't wrap my mind around is the fact that you went back." He grabbed a plant and threw it against the wall. Dirt and pottery spilled onto the floor. "You fucking went back!"

I stood up, but I felt myself get dizzy and sat down. I really needed to eat something. Donovan's expression changed from mad to concerned, then back to mad when he realized that I was okay.

"He's a coward. Why didn't he come to me face to face? Why did he have to call me?"

I saw a change in his eyes, letting me know that the meeting would've only ended one way, making me happy that they didn't meet. Flashes of red and blue lights, sirens and hospital waiting rooms caused a chill to come over me.

"Donovan, what would that have proved? That's juvenile."

"You want to talk about mature?"

"What am I missing?" I asked.

"You don't get it, do you?"

"I guess I don't. I told you that it's over, that I want to make this marriage work."

He gave me a sarcastic laugh, like he was insulted by my new revelation. He asked me how he was supposed to live with me knowing the truth.

"How am I supposed to watch your stomach grow with life without constantly wondering if it's mine?"

I stood up and reached for him, but he stepped away. He didn't want me touching him.

He sighed and turned away from me. He didn't want me to see the fire in his eyes being put out with the tears that were now in them. But I did.

The guilt was killing me—killing us.

He looked at me. I saw the man I fell in love with. The man who kept me out dancing until dawn, and loved me until the sun went down again.

I wanted to go to him, but I didn't have the energy. He looked heavy, as heavy as I felt.

"I don't want a divorce, Donovan."

He sat down, head in hands, and let out a sigh.

"I don't know, Teri."

I couldn't stop them; the tears came. I found myself trying to convince my husband not to leave me and promising things would get better. I told him that now that I was not working full time, we could work on our marriage and becoming a family.

He looked at me, intensity all over his face.

He asked, "Is it over?"

"Yes. What do I have to do to prove that to you?"

I felt like I had been thrust into a time warp. I was back to the day we separated because of Tracie. So much hate and hurt settled in us that day. So many promises had been broken by my husband, seen and unseen, and now, here we were again, only this time because of me.

"I don't know, Teri. I can't commit to what you are asking me if this isn't done with that nigga."

"It is."

"Were you going to leave me?"

That question stunned me. I wasn't expecting it and he knew it. He did it on purpose to get an honest response from me.

"Donovan, it wasn't like that."

"Teri, just answer the question."

"Donovan, I—"

He shook his head slowly. "Wow."

Just like that, he was gone. The soft click of the door snapped me out of my trance.

My husband had just walked out on me.

The tears came in huge waves, waves so big they brought me to my knees. My sobs shook my body so violently I began to fear for my unborn child. I looked at the door through watery vision and force myself to stand. I walked to the front door hoping that he was sitting in his car in the driveway, but my short walk yielded disappointment.

My husband was gone.

Chapter Thirty

The next morning, I walked around in a daze, like I was being controlled by a video game. I forced myself to eat a breakfast of eggs and toast. I was able to swallow two mouthfuls of orange juice before I felt like I wanted to vomit. At noon, I was in my doctor's office getting a checkup. I told the nurse the reason I was by myself was because my husband had to work.

"Would you like to hear the heartbeat?"

I gave her a weak smile and just nodded.

She instructed me to lay back and proceeded to expose my stomach. After putting a warm gel on my abdomen, she ran the monitor around until the tiny sound filled the room, bringing tears to my eyes.

"Sounds good," she said, smiling.

On the way home, I called Renee and cried to her. I told her I was scared of what was to come. I was scared at the prospect of being a single parent. Renee already knew everything. After Donovan walked out, I called her. I knew she would be there for me because that was what friends did. I told her everything and she didn't judge me. She just told me I needed to calm down, if not for me, then for my baby.

When I woke up that morning, there was a note taped to the refrigerator telling me that Donovan needed time to digest things and would be staying at a hotel so he could clear his head.

I dialed his cell, but it went straight to voicemail.

I call his office, but his secretary told me he was in a meeting. I yelled things at her that made her put me on hold, and the next voice I heard was my husband's. I paced the kitchen while rubbing circles on my stomach. I was trying to stay calm as he told me he wasn't sure what he wanted anymore.

"Teri, I thought it was you and our marriage, but this pregnancy is just a constant kick in the ass, reminding me of what happened."

"So this is your way of moving on, leaving?"

"I'm not leaving, Teri. I don't know what I am doing."

"Donovan, you can't leave me like this. I am pregnant. What am I supposed to do?"

"Teri, you have my numbers. You will be fine."

I screamed at him; things that didn't make sense, some that did. I slammed the phone down, missing the base and causing the battery to pop out.

An hour later, Renee was sitting across from me, looking at the note he left me.

"What are you gonna do?"

"I don't know. What do you think I should do?"

She touched my trembling hand. "Give him time, Teri. He'll come around."

"How much time, Renee? I am just ready for this to be over."

"It's not that simple, Teri. You both have done some stupid things, and you have to face it for what it is. Your marriage may not survive this. Are you ready for that?"

I blew out some air and thought about what she said. I wasn't ready for that. When you let emotions and anger fuel you, rather than good judgment, you can almost guarantee a bad outcome.

"He knows that I was going to leave him."

"But you didn't."

I didn't say anything. Instead, I just thought about the way I considered leaving him for Sean, thought about leaving him for myself. Guilt washed over me.

She said, "Look, you have to accept this for what it is right now. You have a baby to worry about. And your baby needs you to be healthy and stable minded."

I smiled at her references to the life growing inside of me. Hearing the heartbeat made it all too real for me.

"I still can't believe I am going to have a baby."

She giggled. "I know! I am excited."

"Why are you excited?"

"I wanted Christopher to be a girl. Hell, you can't dress up little boys."

"Okay, what makes you so sure it's a girl?"

"It has to be, because I want a little girl."

We laughed, her a little more than me, and hugged the kind of hug where a friend reassures a friend that everything will work out and even if it doesn't, she will be there to help pick up the pieces.

We went shopping and laughed for a few more hours before I made my way home with three bags full of baby clothes from Macy's and a pair of Manolo Blahnik shoes just in case my feet ever made it back to their normal size.

When I put my new shoes in the closet, I noticed that a lot of Donovan's things were missing. He had come by when I was gone and started his amputation from my life. His razors were missing, along with his shaving cream, toothbrush, and all of his suits. They were all gone.

I sat on the bed, closed my eyes, and took a deep breath. I couldn't let this get to me.

I had to hold myself together, for my baby, if nothing else.

No matter who her father was, she was mine.

Chapter Thirty-one

My week was one from hell.

It was hard to sleep in that house without Donovan. The house had more creaking and squeaks than a worn-out box spring in a hooker's house. Most of the time, I was able to drink a cup of tea in order to fall asleep, but not last night. I was restless, and worried about Donovan. He hadn't been returning my calls and that wasn't like him, but I guess we had both turned into two different people.

That night, I sat on the edge of my bed and dialed Donovan's number a hundred times in my mind. In my mind, we talked. Sometimes it was civil, with him promising to come home. Other times it was an argument where we yelled and screamed until we were exhausted. In other conversations, we said nothing, but our silence said everything.

I picked up the phone. Held it in my hand, and prayed to a God who I hoped was still listening as I got ready to dial my husband. Before I could, the phone rang, causing me to jump. I laughed at myself and answered it.

"Hello?"

Silence.

"Hello?"

More silence.

I hung up and dialed Donovan's cell. His voicemail came on, so I left him a message.

"Hi. I was just calling. I miss you. Please call me back."

I made my way downstairs. The house seemed too big; too quiet without my husband.

I went into the kitchen and checked the locks on the patio doors before programming 911 into the speed dial on my phone. Donovan had mentioned us getting a dog a while ago; tonight, I wished I had taken him up on his offer. I made my way to the den—to Donovan's space. It smelled like him. I inhaled him in as I looked around the room. His bookshelf was piled high with his books from college. He always said he was going to clean it up and make it look neat, but never got around to it. I walked over to his chair and I sat in it. The leather had molded to his body, and it felt good as it wrapped itself around mine. I leaned back and closed my eyes. I wondered what would become of our marriage.

As I made my way to check the lock on my front door, a knock on the door interrupted my thoughts. The silhouette standing on the other side of the glass door looked all too familiar. I stopped short in the hall and stared at him as he stared back at me through the etched glass door. Fear had planted me in my spot with deep roots. I couldn't move and he knew it.

I saw the knob on the front door turning, but before I could find my legs, it was too late.

Sean was in my house.

Chapter Thirty-two

"What are you doing here?"

"I came to see you."

"You shouldn't be here," I said, trying not to act scared.

"Why?"

"Because, Donovan will be here any minute."

I didn't want to raise my voice and set him off even more.

He slowly started toward me. "No, he won't."

I started walking backward, hoping I could make it to the kitchen and out the patio doors.

"I know that Donovan left," he said. "He's staying at the Georgian Terrace, right?"A smile crept across his face that almost made my heart stop. His eyes were wild and his clothes were disheveled—like he had been in a fight. I saw what appeared to be blood on his shirt. He had something in his hand, but I couldn't make out what it was.

"Please, Sean, just tell me, where is my husband?" I asked calmly, but the fear inside of me was threatening to choke me. I had to get some control or this situation was gonna go from bad to worse real quick.

"Don't worry about him! You need to be worried about me right now and how we're gonna fix this relationship."

I cut my eyes and looked toward the bottom step. I gauged the distance and tried to decide if upstairs or outside was my best chance.

"Sean, you don't have to do this. Let's just sit down and talk."

"Talk?" He shot me a look like he hated me. "You wanna talk?" His voice began to rise. "After what you did to me?"

"Sean, I—"

The house phone rang out, distracting him and giving me my opportunity. I bolted for the steps, but he caught me, causing me to fall. I twisted my body to protect my belly, and screamed out as my knee slammed into the step. At that moment, my only thoughts were of my baby. I managed to shake my foot free and scramble up the steps, but he was right behind me as I bolted into the bedroom and slammed the door closed, locking it.

"Teri! Open the damn door!"

My breathing was ragged and I felt like I was going to pass out. I picked up the phone on the nightstand, but there was no dial tone. I immediately realized that my cell phone was downstairs in my purse. I tossed the home phone against the door.

"Sean, please! Please don't do this."

"Open the door! You and your bitch-ass husband owe me."

I cried so hard I felt like my chest was going to pop. "What are you talking about? Donovan hasn't done anything to you."

The wooden bedroom door jumped behind the force of what had to be him kicking it in. I ran to the bathroom and dug in one of the drawers until I found one of Donovan's razors. I could tell from the sound of the door it wasn't going to stand up to much more of his abuse.

I thought about pushing the dresser in front of

the door, but it was too heavy. Just when I was about to move the lounge chair, the door flew off the hinges, causing me to fall back on the bed.

Sean looked like a man possessed. He lunged toward me, and I tried to scramble to the other side of the bed. He caught me and we both tumbled onto the floor. I scooted to the other side of the room, and when I looked up, he had a gun pointed at me.

"Sean, please," I cried. "I'm pregnant."

"I don't want to hurt you, Teri. Why would you think that?"

I held my hands up, palms out. "Just tell me where Donovan is and then we can talk, okay? I promise."

"I told you not to worry about him. I took care of him." He looked around the room and laughed a little. "You know, I must say, you surprised me. You hung in a lot longer than I thought you would."

I looked at him saw him through confused eyes. "What are you talking about?"

"I mean, after I sent you that package laying out how your husband *fucked* my wife for almost a year, I figured you would leave him, but you didn't."

At that moment, I couldn't breathe. Terror wrapped itself around my body and squeezed so tight I thought my lungs would pop. I shook my head back and forth like I was trying to wake up from a nightmare.

"Oh . . . my . . . God."

He smiled a sadistic smile. "Suprise!"

"All this time? It was you?" I asked. "The pictures—the phone calls. You attacked me in the garage?" I shook my head. "This can't be. This isn't right."

He laughed a little. "No, it wasn't right for your husband to tear apart my marriage. I just figured I'd return the favor, but I had no idea you'd be dumb enough to stay."

"So all this time it's been about Donovan," I said, keeping my eye on his trigger finger.

He got up and made his way over to me. His eyes softened. "At first it was, but then I fell in love with you, Teri. And I know you fell in love with me."

I slowly shook my head, all the while keeping one eye on the gun and the other on him. "Sean, I love my husband. What we did was wrong. We can't be together. It's just not realistic."

"Don't say that!" His hand flew up and caught me across my right cheek, splitting it open. I felt the warm blood run down my face as I cried out. His blow jarred something inside of me, and I knew I had to protect myself and my unborn child.

"I . . . I'm sorry," I stammered, trying to stay calm. "Look, just put the gun down and we can talk."

He raised the gun again and pointed at me. "I'm done talking."

I held up my hands. "Okay, okay. We don't have to talk if you don't want to."

He tilted his head and looked at me like he was confused. "Why are you playing with my mind?"

I shook my head. "No, no. I promise, I'm not. I just want to talk, that's all."

"You hurt me, Teresa, just like Darienne."

"Darienne?"

He looked at me like I was agitating him further. "Darienne. My *wife*!"

"Wait, I thought her name was Tracie."

He let out a slight laugh. "No, that's the bitch's middle name."

My mind hit rewind back to the day Eva gave me the message. "It was someone named Darienne," she'd said.

Oh . . . my . . . God. His wife had been trying to call me. Probably to warn me.

And I never returned her call.

I wiped the blood-stained tears from my cheeks. "I never meant for any of this to happen, Sean, I swear.

Please, we can work this out. We were both hurt. I understand how you're feeling."

I kept one eye on him and the other on the gun. I watched as he lowered it slightly. He ran his other hand over his head. I kept working on him mentally.

"You were betrayed, and that is wrong. But what we did wasn't the answer to either of our problems. This could've been handled differently. And I am so sorry for the part I played in all of this."

For a moment, it looked like he wanted to cry. "Teri, this isn't how this was supposed to happen. You weren't supposed to stay with him." He talked to me, but stared at the wall. "He destroyed my marriage, and I wanted to destroy his."

I slid my hand along my thigh and felt for the blade. "I understand, but you have to let go of your anger. Look what it's doing to you, Sean. Don't allow what Tracie did to destroy you. You're a good person, a good doctor."

"Don't say her name!" he screamed, causing me to jump and lose track of the blade. "That bitch got what she deserved."

"What are you talking about? Where is she?"

"After your husband tossed her ass back, she came crying back to me, and I sent that bitch back to New York with only the clothes on her back!"

Donovan had told me the truth after all. He tried to tell me she was no longer in Atlanta, but I wouldn't listen. It really was over between Donovan and Tracie. I whispered to myself. "Oh my God, what have I done?"

The sound of glass breaking came from downstairs, distracting Sean long enough for me to get the razor from under my leg. I swung my hand, bringing the blade down on his forearm, spilling bright red blood all over both of us. He jumped back and dropped the gun. I jumped up and bolted toward what used to be my bedroom door and ran down the steps.

He was right behind me.

Just as I got to the kitchen, Donovan was coming through the back door. He looked like he had been in a fight. I realized that Donovan and Sean must've gotten into a fight. That's where the blood on Sean's shirt came from.

I had never been happier to see anyone. I really thought something had happened to, him and it affected me more than I realized.

Donovan bolted toward me, but suddenly froze in his tracks. I turned and saw Sean standing behind me with his gun pointed at both of us. We all stood there for a second, no one saying anything. My husband's body was stiff.

I finally said, "What do you want from us, Sean?"

Sean looked at my husband, but talked to me. "I want what he took from me," he said, pointing the gun in Donovan's direction.

"Sean, please. Just listen to me." I slowly stepped into the path between the gun and my husband. I wanted Sean's full attention. "You can't only blame Donovan for this. Your wife is to blame as well. We were all hurt, but killing my husband is not the answer."

He looked toward Donovan. "How does it feel to know your wife got fucked by another man?"

Donovan clenched his jaw. "Teri, go outside."

I started to move toward the door.

Sean trained the gun on me. "She's not going anywhere."

Donovan starting moving toward Sean. His voice was full of anger. "Nigga, point that gun at me! Not my wife!"

I screamed, "Donovan, no!"

I saw what was about to happen, yet I was powerless to stop it. Donovan made the first move, and before I could scream, my husband and my lover were locked onto each other like two lions fighting to protect their pride.

Chapter Thirty-three

Glass shattered as they fell into the kitchen table, knocking it and everything on it to the floor.

"Teri, get out of here!" Donovan demanded.

I heard the sound of sirens coming from outside. Everything was a blur as my house filled with men in blue. I felt someone pulling at me, trying to get me out of the middle of the mayhem. Like two angry pit bulls, Sean and Donovan were locked on each other, determined to draw first blood.

The cops finally pried them apart, and Donovan emerged from the chaos. He looked like a man possessed as his eyes locked on mine. So much hurt and pain lived in his eyes. My mouth was hanging open, but nothing was coming out. I wanted to scream for him, but I couldn't.

I saw Sean. He was bleeding from his mouth and head as the cops wrestled with him.

I kept my eyes on my husband as he started across the room.

Sean continued to fight against his arrest and yell at my husband, but Donovan didn't acknowledge him. He just continued to walk in my direction. As he got closer, his face softened. I tried to make my way to my husband, but I stopped in my tracks when I saw the flash and heard the explosion of a gun come from Sean's direction.

My scream was endless as it shook my body.

Donovan stopped in his tracks and his large frame collapsed. I tried to get to him, but an officer was shielding me. Officers were yelling—telling Sean to drop it. I heard more screaming, then two more shots. I was surrounded by so many people I couldn't see anything, but I didn't have to see to know that Sean was dead.

Later, the bright lights of the ER added fuel to the fire that had become my headache. Renee sat next to me in the waiting room, her arm wrapped around me as she tried to stop my shakes and tremors.

She kept telling me to calm down, while nurses kept trying to examine me.

"Dr. McCall, please let us at least put you on a fetal monitor."

I snapped at the scraggly nurse standing next to me and told her where she could shove her monitor.

"I am not going anywhere until I hear from my husband's doctor."

She sucked her teeth, mumbled something, and marched back to wherever the hell she came from.

Renee glared at me. "You really need to calm down, Teri."

"Why haven't I heard from the doctor? What is going on with my husband?"

She touched my hand. "No news is good news."

"It's taking too long, Renee. What if—what if he's—"

"Don't even think like that. The nurse said that he was awake and talking when they brought him in. I'm sure he's fine."

I felt my sanity slipping away, as I tried to control my breathing.

I had screwed up in a huge way, and now I was going to have to pay the price. Renee grabbed my hand and told me to close my eyes. I did as she said, and the next sound I heard was the soothing sound of her voice . . . praying.

She was asking God to help us, asking him to forgive my husband and me for things I couldn't find the strength to ask forgiveness for on my own. She asked Him to give my husband the strength to pull through this nightmare. She even asked Him to forgive Sean.

Tears came from me, from a place that I didn't know I owned—a spiritual place. With my tears, I felt a cleansing as calm washed over me. For the first time in a long time, I really felt God was listening.

I finally agreed to go to labor and delivery and have my baby monitored. Renee stayed with me while they got me settled in a room. She promised that she would keep watch and let me know as soon as she heard anything about Donovan.

My baby's heart rate was between 120 and 140. Perfect. I watched the blip on the screen and listened to her bump around on the monitor. I drank some juice and munched on some crackers. It was part of the stress test for the baby. To make sure she was responsive, I was supposed to eat sugars to stimulate her. My baby's heartbeat sounded like a tiny washing machine. I listened as I watched the small clock on the wall.

I thought about Sean and hated that he had to die. My heart ached for him in a pitiful sort of way.

He never recovered from finding out that his wife was cheating on him. She wanted to work it out after Donovan broke it off with her, but he couldn't let go of his anger. He had been plotting against us all this time.

It had been almost an hour since Renee left, and I still hadn't heard anything from her or Donovan's doctor. I drifted into an unwanted sleep. I tried to fight it, but it was stronger than I was at that moment.

When I opened my eyes, I blinked against the overhead light above my bed. I pulled a string, and the light went off. The small room was too cool. I looked at the monitor. The baby must have been sleeping because her heart rate had slowed. It was hovering around 120 beats per minute.

The clock told me that almost four hours had passed since the nightmare took place.

I rolled over and looked for the buzzer for the nurse. As I fumbled with the wires that were tangled and going everywhere, the remote hit the floor.

"You need some help?"

The voice sent chills from head to toe and back again.

"Donovan," I whispered.

He was in a wheelchair and Renee was behind him, pushing him. His shoulder was in a sling, and a hospital gown had replaced his blue Ralph Lauren shirt. He had a bruise on the cheek under his left eye.

Renee smiled as she pushed my husband to my bedside.

She said, "He wouldn't let them put him in his room until he saw you."

He asked, "Are you okay?"

"I'm fine. Are you okay?"

"I am now."

I reached over and touched the arm that was in the sling. I ran my fingers over the outline of his forearm and looked into his eyes. Tears filled them.

We talked without talking, apologizing for so many things without speaking. I gave him all the love I had to offer, and he took it willingly. We got lost in each other and the moment.

He asked, "How's the baby?"

"She's fine." I smiled.

He became fascinated with the monitor and the sound of her heart beating, pumping hope into the room.

"I love you, Teri," he said, touching my swollen belly. "No matter what."

"I love you too, Donovan. No matter what."

I didn't notice Renee slip out, leaving Donovan and me to start to pick up the pieces of our marriage.

Epilogue

With a lot of counseling and a renewed commitment to our marriage, we never mentioned Sean again. He would always hold a spot in our hearts, in that place where we kept all of the mysteries of "what could've been" tucked away to flip through when no one is around. For those moments when you wonder, what could've been if you didn't get married? What could've been if you majored in something else? What could've been if you had followed your mind instead of your heart?

The bullet hit Donovan in the shoulder. The doctor said it was clean; in and out with no permanent damage. The hours that we were apart and I didn't know what was going on gave me a real dose of my own "what could've been." And I didn't like it.

Eventually the holidays swallowed us, allowing us to heal in its warm arms. We spent Thanksgiving with Renee and her family, and got to talk to Derrick via speakerphone from Germany. Christmas was quiet. We spent it at home, just the two of us. We exchanged gifts in front of our tree. Donovan gave me a gift certificate to Spa Sydell for a prenatal massage session and weekly massage sessions after the baby was born.

I even received a gift from Mr. Wendell: a picture of him and the clown at his nephew's birthday party, along with a thank you note attached. I left the practice, deciding to focus on making my life better, concentrating on my husband and my daughter. We even started attending Renee's church on Sundays. We both developed a renewed strength in God. It took this harrowing experience for us to realize that our marriage would not—could not—make it without Him.

Donovan would get his gift from me that spring, in the form of a baby girl, who had her mother's nose and her father's beautiful Latin eyes.

About the Author

D.L. Sparks is a native of Pittsburgh, PA, but now resides outside of Atlanta. D.L. is a contributing author in the 2007 anthology, Erogenous Zone: A Sexual Voyage, with her short story entitled "Keystrokes." When she is not writing, she spends time with her family and friends, likes to travel, and is an avid reader. She is currently working on her next novel.